DUSTY AYRES AND HIS BATTLE BIRDS:
THE PURPLE TORNADO

THE PURPLE TORNADO

By *Robert Sidney Bowen*

ALTUS PRESS • 2017

EDITED AND DESIGNED BY

Matthew Moring

PUBLISHING HISTORY

"The Purple Tornado" originally appeared in the September, 1934 (Vol. 6, No. 2) issue of *Dusty Ayres and his Battle Birds* magazine. Copyright 2017 by Steeger Properties, LLC. All rights reserved.

CHAPTER 1
BLACK CHALLENGE

"**A**ND IN recognition of valuable services rendered, the President and the Congressional War Council hereby appoint you special contact officer to the combined armed forces of the U.S. Government. In the carrying out of this emergency roving commission, you are hereby permitted to act independently of any branch of the three major services, and report your findings direct to the General Staff at Washington, D.C. Notice of this appointment appears in general order number ZY 679.

"Signed, the President, and chairman of the C.W.C."

Deftly folding the official document, Colonel Marberry, acting chief of staff, dropped it on the desktop and reached out his big right paw.

"Let me be the first to congratulate you, Captain Ayres," he smiled at the lean, wind-bronzed pilot. "I am sincerely happy that our Government has seen fit to place this trust upon your capable shoulders."

Saluting stiffly, Dusty Ayres, top eagle of Uncle Sam's brood, grasped the colonel's hand and shook it firmly.

"Thank you, sir," he stammered. "I only hope that I shall always be able to prove myself worthy of this great honor."

"I'm sure you will, my boy," smiled the senior officer with genuine pleasure.

And then he turned to the third man in the group office, Major Drake, C.O. of High Speed Group No. 7.

"As Captain Ayres' former commanding officer, you are to be congratulated, too, Major. And now, if you'll both excuse me, I'll be getting on back. No, don't bother; my car is right outside. Good day, gentlemen."

When the door closed, Dusty whistled softly, dropped into the nearest chair, and drew a hand across his forehead.

"Gosh!" he ejaculated.

Major Drake chuckled and placed a hand on the pilot's shoulder.

"Wouldn't believe me, would you, eh?" he grunted. "Well, it's just as I predicted. You're a one-man army now, son. You can tell your old C.O. to go fly a kite, and he'd have to take it. General staff is your boss, now."

Dusty swallowed hard, struggled to his feet.

"Listen, Major," he blurted out as the red seeped up his neck. "I've been under your command for two years, and—er—well, this—"

The C.O.'s tightening fingers on his shoulder stopped him.

"Hold it, son," said Major Drake. "I understand what you're trying to say. You don't want to cut away from the old gang? Well, you won't be cutting away. Your drome will be any one of the hundred from Duluth to the Atlantic coast. If you want to operate out of this field, then that'll be swell. But you've been given a grave responsibility. In a way, you've been appointed, on the President's order, as Flying Trouble Shooter Number One. You rate it, so don't let any thoughts about the old homestead cramp your style. There isn't one of us who isn't tickled silly about your receiving this honor. So do your stuff, and remember that the old candle will be burning in the window for you, any time you drop in."

Dusty grinned and ran the tip of his tongue over his lower lip.

"Don't worry, sir, I won't forget," he said, huskily. "Only—well, I suppose I should do a jig or something, but somehow I feel like a fellow bailing out at midnight. Don't know just where I'm going to land."

"You'll find out soon enough, if past events mean anything," Major Drake chuckled. "Ever since Fire-Eyes and his damned Black Invaders started banging on our front door, action has come to you like a steel chip to a magnet. You haven't had to wait for anything."

At that moment, as though in confirmation of the statement, the door opened and the field signal officer came charging inside. He walked quickly over to Dusty and thrust out a radiogram.

"For you, skipper!" he panted. "What the hell do you make of that?"

Dusty took the paper and stared at the typed message.

To Captain Ayres,
High Speed Group Seven.

My congratulations on your new appointment. It would seem that I have underestimated your true worth, or else your country has overestimated it. However, I suggest that we settle the matter by meeting each other at twenty thousand feet over your northeastern area map position M-18. As I have important mission to fulfill later I would like to take care of this affair between ten-thirty and eleven o'clock, this morning.

In the event that you do not meet me I will consider my belief to be correct that your government has been misguided by the sheer good fortune that has befallen a blundering fool.

The Black Hawk.

"Oh, yeah?" echoed Dusty in a hard voice as he finished reading. Then to the signal officer, "When the hell did this come through?"

"Not over five minutes ago," was the prompt answer. "It was sent direct on the station's official wave-length. From Black station KZ in the Ontario Zone, too. The bums even asked for a check-back and reply in half an hour."

Dusty glanced at his watch. The hands showed twenty-four minutes after nine.

"Okay on the check-back," he nodded grimly. "Shoot the flash along to him that I'll be there with bells on!"

"You really mean you're—?"

"Damned tooting!" Dusty cut him off. "I wouldn't miss this for a flock of steak dinners. Scram, Sparky, old kid."

The signal officer shot him a searching look, shrugged and turned on his heel.

"Okay, Skipper," he grunted over his shoulder. "I'll take vanilla, myself!"

The pilot laughed and turned to the C.O.

"Guess you called the turn again, major," he grinned. "Here

I'm wondering just how I'm going to start this new job of mine, and pop!—the first move drops right into my lap."

Drake snorted, scowled at the floor.

"I don't like it!" he growled.

"Don't like it?" Dusty echoed. "Hell, I love it! Nothing would suit me better than to plant that flying rat down under, once and for all. I've tangled with him so many times, I'm getting sick of the sight of his homely mug. And besides—"

He paused and pointed through the Group office window toward the Silver Flash II resting on the tarmac.

"And besides," he repeated a moment later, "it'll be a swell chance to see how my new bus shapes up in action. Incidentally, I don't think I've thanked you yet, sir, for rushing through the request for my new ship. She's a honey. Never expected to fly anything better than the crate I lost in that Washington scrap, but she's that and then some. Why, only this morning I got five-sixty-eight m.p.h. out of her, and—"

"I know, I know!" the other cut in gruffly. "It's the last word in planes, and all the rest of it. But listen, Ayres, this Black Hawk is no damned fool."

"That's right," nodded Dusty. "Just conceited. And I'm the fair-haired boy who is going to shoot it out of him. If you knew him like I do, major, you'd—"

"I'd wonder what was behind his challenge," the C.O. finished sharply. "You're a better man than he is. You've beat him to the punch half a dozen times. Watch your step, it may be a trap. You're no match for the whole Black Invader air force, you know."

Dusty shrugged, pulled out a pack of cigarettes, offered the major one and took one himself.

"Right again, sir," he said as he held a match for them both. "But here's a stepping-off place for this new title the President has handed me. The Hawk is the head of the Black air force. We hate each other's guts, and getting him will hand the rest of his vultures a jolt they won't like. Maybe it is a trap, and maybe there's something bigger behind it than just a two-ship scrap. Well, that'll be okay, too. I've at least got a starter, and that's all I want."

The C.O. spewed smoke ceiling-ward and nodded.

"You don't have to tell me that," he muttered. "Well, remember, you've got a radio and there's eighteen planes here that'll come a-flying if it should turn out to be a trap. Meantime, I'll buzz Washington to start checking on how the hell the Blacks heard about your new appointment before even our own troops did."

For a moment Dusty's face went grave.

"Yeah, that's so, isn't it?" he murmured. "Oh, well, as General Horner of Intelligence once said, there's a Black agent behind every lamppost in Washington. But if their finding it out caused the Hawk to get up enough steam to send me this invite, then three cheers for them! Well, so long, sir. I'll be seeing you soon!"

A quick salute and Dusty hard-heeled out of the Group office and went over to his plane. Two minutes later he was pulling clear and streaking up for altitude.

NOT ONCE did he look down back at the familiar sight below. Like the knights of old who set out alone to seek their destiny in distant lands, so was this modern warrior of the skies riding his thundering charger into the great unknown. Life and death rode the cockpit with him, and on his broad shoulders rested the responsibility of his own fate, whatever it might be.

For a moment memory of the glorious days and nights spent with High Speed Group No. 7 caused the instrument panel to blur before his eyes. Then he laughed and slammed his free fist against the bulletproof side of his cockpit.

"It's just the dish you ordered, kid!" he shouted aloud. "Responsible only to general staff—if and when! Yip-p-y!"

Heart pounding with wild joy, and the blood dancing through his veins, he hand-heeled the throttle wide open, booted the plane around on wingtip and sent it roaring across the Massachusetts line and straight up the border of Vermont and New Hampshire.

A glance at the magnetic clock on the dash showed the time to be ten-seventeen. Checking his position on the roller map he nosed up through a cloud layer and didn't level off until the altimeter needle quivered at the twenty-one thousand foot mark.

Then he eased back to half throttle, let the ship have its head, and keenly studied the heavens in all directions. To his eagle eye there came not a single sight of anything, except clouds and pale blue emptiness.

Several minutes later he grinned, spun the wave-length dial and unhooked the transmitter tube.

"Calling Ontario Station KZ!" he shouted. "Captain Ayres speaking. Please reply to the commander of your air force that

I'm waiting. He is five minutes late already. Has black changed to yellow?"

Without waiting to get a check-back on his call, he slipped the transmitter back on the hook, and continued his searching study of the surrounding sky. Minutes dragged by. The hands of the dash clock swung around to ten forty-six—and still he had the heavens all to himself.

At eleven o'clock, exactly, he suddenly hunched forward on the seat and stared hard toward the northern horizon. The silver cloud layer was slowly changing to a murky blue-gray in color.

As he watched, the color deepened to a dirty purple and a great billowing curtain of the stuff rose straight up from the cloud layer. Higher and higher it rose until its pluming crest was lost in the sub-stratosphere regions.

"By God, that's a gas curtain!"

Even as Dusty muttered the words aloud, the red signal light on the radio panel blinked, and a voice crackled in the phones clamped to his ears.

"All American planes in northeastern zone, attention! Enemy releasing gas curtain from position N-27 to Z-10. All pilots not equipped with protectors will keep ten miles clear of this area. Winds generally northwest from ground to thirty-five thousand feet. Maximum velocity eighteen. Minimum, five miles. Stand by for all clear signal if you are flying enemy territory patrols."

As the ground station started to repeat, Dusty tuned down the volume and studied his roller map. The result brought a puzzled frown to his brows. He raised his eyes toward the massive purple curtain hanging in the sky. It seemed to be slowly moving away from him—away toward the northwest.

"Hell!" he gasped. "The blacks must be nuts. That damned thing is swinging back over their own lines! God, this is screwy!"

Sliding the cockpit cowl shut and turning the sealing clamps, he adjusted the air pressure equalizer and nosed the Silver Flash II toward the purple curtain.

But when he was still a good five miles from it, he suddenly pulled up in a screaming zoom and swung around toward the west.

A jet-black monoplane had plunged out of the curtain of gas and was streaking due south. In one flash look, Dusty saw the Black Invader insignia on its fuselage—a black flag edged in white. A shout of battle spilled off his lips.

"Showed up at last, eh?" he shouted. "Hey, over this way, bum! Here I am!"

But the other ship did not alter its course a single inch. Like a winged black arrow it kept right on slicing southward.

Belting the stick and booting the rudder, Dusty spun his plane around and charged after it.

"Just like that, huh?" he snorted. "Well, maybe this will attract your attention!"

He slid his thumbs up to the electric trigger trips as he spoke, started to jab them forward, then suddenly jerked his thumbs away. From a good ten thousand feet above his altitude, two more Black ships were piling down toward the first, their guns slanting twin streams of jetting flame down across the sky.

Wide-eyed, Dusty watched them streak earthward; saw them

close the gap in a period of split seconds and rake the first plane from prop to tail wheel with fire-spitting guns.

A MOMENT later, action was preceding the thought in his brain. Hardly realizing what he was doing, he cut around in a screaming half turn, yanked the nose up and hurled the Silver Flash II straight at the attacking planes.

The range was too great, and for the first few moments, their pilots ignored him. But as he roared in close, the nearest one slanted off and came rushing right at him.

Eyes hard, lips curled back in a savage grin, Dusty steadied his ship and took deliberate aim. And then steel fury swirled out from the muzzles of his Brownings and buried itself in the vitals of the Black ship.

For an instant it seemed as though the onrushing plane had stopped dead in its tracks. Then it lurched crazily to the side and hovered almost motionless for a split second before it went cork-screwing upward.

Relentlessly, Dusty followed it up, hammering it from prop to fin with burst after burst of singing steel. No creation of man could have withstood the devastating fire that spewed out from Dusty's guns, and the upward spinning Black monoplane was no exception.

A thousand feet higher and both wings wrenched free and went slip-sliding off like dried leaves. The rest curved over like a spent rocket, and went racing down, over-revving engine howling a song of certain doom.

As it streaked by, Dusty strained his eyes for a glimpse of the figure in the glass-cowled cockpit. But if he expected to see the cruel hatchet face of the Black Hawk, he was disappointed. All he could see were the head and shoulders of a black-uniformed figure slumped forward against the instrument panel.

And then, as he jerked his eyes away, he promptly forgot all about the thing. The second Black plane had fired the fuel tank of the first plane. It was now little more than a ball of flame and oily black smoke slithering down the skyway.

And the remaining plane was slashing down toward a limp figure in civilian garb who hung suspended at the end of parachute shroud lines.

The same impulse that sent Dusty tearing up toward the two attackers sent him roaring down on the one that remained.

That he should suddenly risk his life to help an unknown at the controls of an enemy plane, he did not try to understand. Something inside of him had sent him charging into the strange sky battle, and that same strange something, fired by additional rage that a helpless figure in parachute harness was being attacked, sent him gun-blazing downward.

But the pilot of the remaining Black ship must have seen him coming, and had no stomach for a possible end such as had been the fate of his companion. After spewing out one final burst at the dangling figure on the shroud lines, he cut off sharply to the west and went swinging round to the north in a furious curving dive.

Dusty started to follow, then checked his ship and swung around toward the limp figure floating earthward.

Throttling a bit, he eased in close and studied the man intently. Friend or foe, he could not tell, for the wind had whipped the front of the figure's jacket up over his face. But as he circled about, wondering, he saw the man stiffly raise his right arm in what was supposed to be a salute.

Then, as though the effort had been too much, the arm dropped down and hung lifeless from its shoulder socket. A few minutes later the swaying figure floated down out of view in a cloud layer.

As it disappeared, Dusty hesitated and glanced at the dash clock. It was twenty-eight minutes after eleven. He looked toward the towering gas curtain far to the north, and made up his mind.

"We'll see this through first," he grunted, and stuck the nose down.

When he came out of the cloud layer it took him a few seconds to pick out the mushroom chute against the earth's carpet. It was several thousand feet below him and sinking toward a hill and rocky section of ground.

A ground wind caught the silk folds of the chute, billowed them out like a sail, and dragged the still figure a good twenty yards before the shroud lines snubbed about a tree trunk.

A moment later he saw the man struggle to his knees, try to continue the rest of the way, and go crashing down on his face.

Noting a small clearing a half mile to his right, Dusty swung toward it, cut the throttle, and slid into it with less than a dozen feet to spare. Slapping open the cowling, he legged out and ran back toward the flapping silk fouled on some heavy underbrush.

First cutting the man loose from the shroud lines, he then turned him over and stared down at the face. It was not a pretty sight. A bullet crease across the forehead was flowing blood freely, that ran down to mingle with the blood from a hundred ugly scrapes and scratches caused by the "wind-drag" across the rocky soil.

Outside of the cuts and scratches the face was of ordinary structure. Its owner might be a member of most any of the white races.

He was of average height, dark brown hair and between twenty and perhaps thirty years of age. The clothes he wore were of general style and material, and tailored to his figure.

All those items Dusty noted in a glance as he put his hand over the man's heart. There was a faint beat, and when he pulled his hand away, it was soaked with blood.

Ripping open the shirt, he jammed his handkerchief in a gaping wound. Bullets had torn half the chest away.

"No—use—thanks."

Blood flecked lips were moving, and pain-filled brown eyes gleamed their gratitude as Dusty looked at the face.

"Take it easy, fellow," he grinned cheerfully. "Just a couple of scratches. I'll get you out. Who are—?"

"No use, flyer," the words seemed to drag themselves off the thin lips. "Finished this time. Listen—tell—attack—Z-10—but—they—right shoe—"

The rest trailed off to a choking gurgle. The man trembled and a mad look came into his eyes. Blood sprayed off the foaming lips as he made a desperate effort to put syllables together.

"Hold it," soothed Dusty, crooking an arm about the man's neck. "Try not to waste your strength."

The eyes blazed at him angrily.

"Shut up! I know I'm finished. Listen, tell—I am—right shoe—right sh—"

The last word was never finished. Dusty felt a wild tremor shoot through the man's body. The eyelids fluttered closed, and the mouth sagged open.

He lowered the man's head and shoulders gently to the ground.

CHAPTER 2
DEAD MAN'S SECRET

FOR SEVERAL moments, Dusty gazed down at the still figure, but death was not to be cheated of its prey. The man was beyond all help on this earth.

Dusty swallowed hard, and began the gruesome task of searching the other's pockets. Each article that he found he placed on the ground beside him.

When he finished, he had two handkerchiefs, a penknife, a length of wrapping twine, seventy cents in Canadian money, a pencil made in Toronto, and two imitation pearl cufflinks. On the inside pocket of the jacket he found a few loose threads where the maker's label had been sewn, but there was no label now.

Further investigation brought to light the fact that even the maker's name on the inside of the shirt neckband had been removed.

Sinking back on his haunches, he fingered the collection of articles.

"If you didn't want anybody to find out," he grunted at the death-chilled face, "you certainly did a damned good job of it!"

And then, suddenly, as his eyes roved over the body, he fastened them on the man's feet and recalled to memory a few of the disconnected words. The man had tried to say something about his right shoe.

Dusty looked at it, and saw nothing unusual. It was neither new nor old. Just a low-cut oxford of ordinary style.

Impulsively, he untied the laces, pulled the shoe off, and examined it closely. The heel was solid, a little probing with the penknife proved that.

He stuck fingers inside the shoe, started to pull them out, and stiffened. Jamming the tongue up through the laces, he shoved his fingers clear to the toe and pecked at a small paper wad that was tightly wedged into the crevice where the toe-cap was joined to the sole. He was unable to dislodge it.

Pulling his hand out, he took the penknife and slashed the toe-cap down the middle. Prying the two sides apart with one hand, he levered out a dirty pellet of paper with the penknife blade.

It was no bigger than the tip of his little finger, and popped out like a marble.

Picking it up he started to unwad it. When he did, a small green bead rolled out into the palm of his hand. The paper that had been wadded about the bead was so dirty and creased and wrinkled that at first he saw nothing on it. In fact, he was about to toss it away when he suddenly gasped and smoothed it out between his palms.

Eyes narrowed, he stared at it intently.

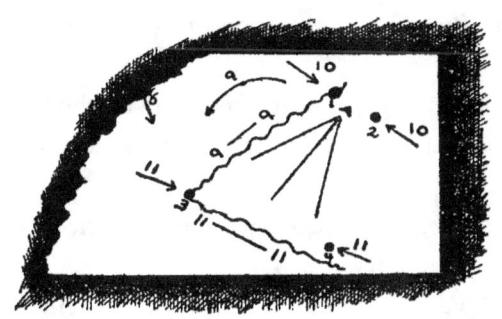

But the more he studied it, the more befuddled he became as to its meanings. As far as he was concerned, it could mean almost anything.

That there had once been more of the cockeyed diagram was evident by the short arrow and the portion of the figure eight at the torn edge of the paper. On the reverse side there was nothing but dirt and sweat marks.

Dusty closed his eyes and tried to remember all that the dying man had said.

The result was partial confirmation of the growing belief that the man was either a Canadian or an American secret agent. He had tried to say something about an attack and Z-10. He—

"By God, Z-10!" Dusty muttered aloud. "That's the northern end of that damned gas curtain!"

Jumping to his feet, he started to go back to his plane for a look at his roller map, when suddenly he stopped in his tracks.

Off to his right something was crashing through the underbrush. Instinctively he shoved the bead and the paper in his pocket, and flicked his other hand to the butt of his service revolver.

But before he could draw it, a beautiful bay horse, with a tall United States artillery major astride its back, came charging into the clearing.

The major swept the scene with a quick glance, dismounted, and came striding forward.

"What the devil's happened, Captain?" he demanded. "Saw this man float down, and saw you circle after him. Who is he?"

Dusty's jaw squared at the other's tone. "I don't know, sir," he said tightly. "That's what I've been trying to find out."

"So I see," said the other dryly. "Were you fighting him in the air? Doesn't look like a Black to me."

Suspicious eyes bored into Dusty's. With an effort, the pilot curbed a hot retort. Instead, he said, "Two Blacks shot at him after he'd jumped. I followed him down, but he died as I reached him."

Dusty started to speak of the man's last words, but on sudden impulse he checked himself. A faint sneer of contempt was curling back the major's lips.

"And you let him be shot down, eh?" he snapped. "A fine business. I suppose the attackers got away? If he was a pilot, why was he wearing civilian clothes?"

The Yank pilot's eyes narrowed and the hardness in his voice matched that of the major's.

"Suppose you answer that?" he grated. "I can't. He was flying a Black plane. The wreck's around this area some place. So is the wreck of one of the attackers. They got him before I could help. I let the other go because this man was coming down by chute, and I was curious."

The major seemed unimpressed.

"Hum-m," he mused. "What's your name?"

The officer's belligerent attitude forced the words off Dusty's tongue before he realized he was speaking them.

"Have you read general order ZY 679, Major?" he bit off.

The artillery-man stiffened and his chin came out.

"Yes, and what the devil's that got to do with it?"

"Nothing, except that I happen to be Captain Ayres!"

The major's chin went back into normal position, his eyes widened a trifle, and he pursed his lips.

"Oh, I see," he grunted. "So, you're *the* Captain Ayres, eh? Then, perhaps, you'll be good enough to tell me in detail about this thing, Captain. I'm Major Walker, acting area commander, and—"

He suddenly stopped short and shot a stiff forefinger at the ground.

"That penknife!" he exclaimed. "Where did you get it?"

WITHOUT WAITING for Dusty's reply, he scooped up the knife. Then dropping to his knees he bent over and peered hard at the dead man. When, a moment later, he straightened up, rage was twisting his features.

"The complete details!" he barked. "I want the *true* story!"

Dusty walked close to him, and his voice was like steel against steel.

"I told you what happened, Major Walker!" he clipped out. "Now suppose you tell me—who is he? You recognized him, just now."

"I most certainly did!" gritted the other, tapping the penknife against his other hand. "He is Charles Strickland, a cousin of mine. I sent him this penknife on his birthday six months ago. And, *five* days ago, I received a letter from him stating that the Army doctor had refused his enlistment because of bad health! *And*, to my knowledge, he never spent a single hour in an airplane, much less to pilot one. His heart was bad."

The inference behind the words started the blood up Dusty's neck.

"Meaning just what, Major?" he asked evenly.

"Meaning that I doubt your story, and that I have no proof that you're who you say you are!"

Dusty started to raise a hand to the group identification card in his tunic pocket, then let it drop as he remembered he never carried it while in the air. Never carried any means of identification, in fact.

"I'm afraid, Major, you'll have to believe both," he said.

The others eyes flickered down to the slashed shoe.

"You cut that shoe!" he snapped. "Why? Did my cousin say something before he died?"

Dusty hesitated, then nodded.

"Yes he did," he replied. "But I am making my report direct

to general staff. And now, if you'll be kind enough to take care of the body, I'll be on my way. I have something to do that can't wait."

Saluting, the pilot turned and started to walk toward his plane.

"Stop right where you are!"

The voice spun him around, an angry retort on his lips. But he didn't say it. The artillery officer had his automatic out, and its muzzle was trained dead on Dusty's heart.

For a second the pilot's jaw dropped in blank surprise. Then berserk rage gripped him, and the sense of courtesy to a superior officer went overboard.

"You damned fool, are you crazy?" he roared. "Put down that gun!"

"Keep your hands still!" the other snarled. "We'll find out just who you are when we get back to headquarters."

With a quick movement, the major stepped forward and jerked Dusty's gun from its holster.

"There, that's better," he grunted, pocketing it. "Now, pick up that body, and walk in front of my horse. One false move and I'll put a bullet in you!"

Dusty curbed his mounting wrath.

"For God's sake, man, listen to me! I've got to fly north and see what the hell that gas curtain is all about. Your cousin said something about an attack. I've got to see the Z-10 C.O."

"Shut up! My cousin wouldn't know anything about an attack. Don't try that on me. If you are Captain Ayres, we'll find out soon enough."

"And G.H.Q. will be down on your neck like a ton of bricks, you fathead!" Dusty blazed.

"Perhaps!" he snapped. "We'll see about that, later. Now, pick him up, and be careful."

Dusty hesitated, went rigid, then relaxed completely.

"Very well," he groaned. "Just as you say, sir."

Bending over the dead man, he reached out his hands, started to curl them about the still form, and then, in a movement faster that the human eye could follow, he whirled and swung up his clenched fist with every ounce of his strength.

In the same movement, he flung out his left hand and knocked the gun down. A bellow of rage spilled off the major's lips, and a split second later it was drowned out as his gun roared flame and sound. But, as the bullet plowed harmlessly into the ground, Dusty's steel-bunched fist caught him under the jaw.

Teeth clicked sharply, the moon-faced head snapped back, and the man's knees buckled. Stepping quickly to one side, Dusty caught the toppling figure and eased him to the ground.

Retrieving his own automatic, he gave the limp artillery officer one last glance.

"Sorry, you fathead," he murmured. "But you asked for it." He turned on his heel and raced back to his plane.

CHAPTER 3
SKY DUEL

W ITH THE same skill and ease with which he slid into the clearing, he slid out of it again, engine wide

22

open and pointed toward the heavens. Holding the ship that way, he looked toward the north.

The curtain of gas still hung in the sky. If anything, it was more dense than before. There was also another change.

The pluming crest was being doubled back northwestward by a high wind, giving it the appearance of a weird, gigantic sail billowed out taut by a gale.

Its length he judged to be well over three hundred miles; clear from the Great Lakes northeast to the northwestern reaches of Maine. Its thickness he could not tell as yet. But as he thundered toward the strange sight he was unable to see a single thing beyond its murky purpleness.

Impulsively he reached out and spun the wave-length dial.

"Captain Ayres calling Area 27 station!" he shouted into the transmitter.

A few seconds later the call-back buzzed in the earphones.

"Twenty-seven on your wave-length! Go ahead!"

"That gas curtain!" said Dusty. "It's getting thicker and blowing back over the enemy lines. What's the ground report on it?"

"The same as before," came the answer. "The enemy have blocked out their entire Front. It is impossible for us to see their movements. We are ready for an attack, but do not expect one. There are no enemy aircraft below the clouds, and no artillery action, either. What's the report from your position, Captain Ayres?"

"No aircraft sighted this side of the curtain," called Dusty. "Will let you know developments, if any. Signing off."

DUSTY'S STEEL-BUNCHED FIST CAUGHT HIM UNDER THE JAW.

Flipping up the wave-length switch, Dusty leaned back against the head rest and stared thoughtfully toward the most northern point of the gas curtain.

"An attack at Z-10, he said, eh?" he mused aloud, turning the roller map. "Now, let's see. Z-10 is where Maine and New Hampshire meet the Canadian line. If they did smash through to the coast they'd bottle up the fifth and sixth armies in Maine. And that would shorten their battle front a couple hundred miles. And—"

He finished the rest with a muttered curse. An attack in the Z-10 area would be suicide for the Black Invaders. He knew that. America had built up a well-nigh impregnable line of defenses at that point.

Almost at the very beginning of the war, Yank G.H.Q. had realized the possibility of an attempt by the enemy to cut off the finger of Maine that stuck up into Canada between the provinces of Quebec and New Brunswick. And to thwart any such attempt a barrier had been built all along the western border of Maine.

Not only that, a great system of rapid transport had been laid down from that point south, so that within the space of twelve hours the might of the entire U.S. Army could be rushed to fill up what few gaps the Blacks might make in the lines.

No, it was foolish to consider a Black offensive in Z-10. Yet—Dusty shrugged and turned the wave-length knob again.

"Calling Z-10 area commander!" he barked into the tube. "Calling Z-10 area commander... emergency. Captain Ayres coming in to land. Please meet me. Have important matter to talk about. Do you get—get my message?"

The panel light blinked almost immediately.

"Message received, Captain Ayres," crackled the earphones. "Do not try to land at Z-10. Area covered by gas. Keep wave-length open for a clear signal."

"Z-10… wait!" he bellowed. "I've got a protector. I can get down all right. Turn your radio beacon on and I'll follow it in."

Anxiously he waited for the needle on the graduated dial on the dash to move, telling him the Z-10 had turned on the beam. But it remained motionless.

With a grunt, he snapped his fingers against the glass, but still the needle did not move.

Puzzled, he called Z-10 for a check-back on his request. But as he did, there came a faint hum in the phones, and an eerie tingle rippled up and down his spine.

Either Z-10 was refusing to receive his wave-length signals, or else some other station was "jamming" the area.

Heeling the throttle all the way open, he climbed up to twenty-five thousand, leveled off, and flew by compass to a point where his wind-speed and drift indicator told him he was directly over the Z-10 area.

Less than half a mile off his left wing was the huge, billowing gas curtain, its crest still curving more and more toward the northwest.

Turning on full radio power, he set the wave adjuster for vertical plane-to-ground station transmission and called Z-10 again.

Tense seconds went by, and then suddenly he heard faint sounds in the earphones. It was like a weak voice trying to yell through a solid brick wall.

Full reception volume brought the voice up a little, but it was too muffled for Dusty to make out. It was followed by a sharp clicking, and then Dusty could understand.

"... and the area commander suggests that you reconnoiter northwest of the gas curtain, if possible. It is believed that preparations are being made for an attack at this point. Please give us a report as soon as possible. Signing off."

Dusty swore and slapped the off switch.

"Was going to do that anyway!" he snorted. "Okay. If you suspect an attack, there's no need of my wasting fuel to land and tell you what little I know."

MAKING SURE that the cowl was sealed, and the air pressure equalizer was set, he swung the Silver Flash II toward the top of the curving gas curtain.

Then, holding the ship steady, he pulled the strange diagram from his pocket and stared at it thoughtfully. None of the markings had changed, and it did not signify anything more to him than it had in the beginning.

"Charles Strickland, eh?" he grunted to himself. "And his cousin, that cluck major, said he wasn't a pilot. I wonder if there were two guys in that single seater? But, hell, this guy told me about his shoe. And—"

He cut off the rest, and started to swing the plane about and head back for Intelligence H.Q. at Washington. Then, with a savage shake of his head, he changed his mind again and swung back north.

"You've got enough to work on, kid, without running home to papa. Take a look around here first."

As his grated words died to an echo in the cowled pit, he shoved the nose down and tore into the murky purple.

When it closed over him he snapped on the dashlight, glued his eyes to the instrument panel, and held the ship in its wild plunge.

Down, down he went—a silver bird cutting through a dark thunderhead. The altimeter needle slid around the graduated dial peg by peg, until at last it was close to the five-thousand foot mark.

The air in the sealed cockpit fogged up a bit, and he was forced to keep his oxygen tube clamped over his nose and mouth.

And then at four thousand, when he was about ready to level off and climb back out of the purple sea that swirled about him, the gas changed to dull gray, and then to faint yellow as he reared down into clean air.

Checking his dive, he swung southwest, rubbed a rag on the fogged-up cowl glass, and stared through it at a panorama of war that made him suck in his breath in sharp gasps.

The ground in every direction was fairly crawling with troops, tanks motor artillery and heavy siege guns. Bomb-proof pill-boxes dotted the ground, and behind them was a crisscross maze of cement and steel—girder reinforcement trenches, with their heavily armored dugouts evenly spaced at intervals of fifty feet.

Behind them thousands of tanks were lined up, their knife-like snouts pointing toward the United States defenses.

At a dozen military rail terminals, long streamlined trains were landing hordes of black, steel-helmeted troops.

And supporting it all were great batteries of naval guns, their muzzles elevated for high trajectory bombardment.

In truth, it was like a world of war all its own, completely hidden beneath the great curtain of purple gas.

One look and Dusty knew beyond all possible doubt that the greatest offensive of all time was about to be launched against Z-10 area. Yet even with all this great array of weapons, the Blacks would never be able to crush the American defenses. Not in a hundred million years. The Yanks in Z-10 were too well prepared. They would be able to hole up and repel any kind of an attack.

"You're crazy, you damned fools!" he muttered as he went sweeping over the countless upturned faces below. "We'll beat hell out of you any day in the week. We'll—"

He heard nothing, and saw nothing, yet that certain thing in every human that science calls a sixth sense, suddenly flashed him an inner warning. He knew, even as he choked off his words and turned in the seat, that he was no longer alone in the air.

And he wasn't.

Racing down out of the drifting canopy of purple gas were a dozen sleek Dart monoplanes of the Black Air Force.

In line formation they came, the two end planes swinging out for a broad-side, cross-fire attack. An instant later Dusty saw the middle ship wobble its wings, and a harsh voice rasped in his earphones.

"Sorry, that I was delayed, Captain Ayres. However, the pleasure is all mine, now!"

The last word was punctuated by a savage burst of jetting flame that leaped out from the pointed snout of the plane. But it was a perfectly good waste of ammunition, for Dusty had instantly recognized the voice of his hated enemy, the Black Hawk, and had flung the Silver Flash up and over in a screaming half roll.

The Hawk's burst of fire was the signal for the others, and like so many flame-spitting demons from Mars, they came roaring in on three sides.

The Silver Flash seemed to almost flinch visibly as the shower of singing steel slashed and tore at its armor plating from prop boss to tail wheel.

Eyes agate, Dusty hurled his plane about in devil-may-care abandonment, and held both trigger trips jammed all the way forward.

There was no time to pick out any one Black plane and charge it. There were too many against him. It was simply a case of making himself as difficult a target as possible, and hope that his twin streams of smoking steel would find their end in something flashing across his sights.

A moment later something did flash across his sights; became a ball of flame and went swirling earthward. He got only a quick glimpse of it, but it fired him with savage joy. First blood for him, anyway!

"Come on!" he roared. "I've got plenty more like it!"

A harsh chuckle in the earphones brought realization that his wave-length was open.

"And a double dose for you, *Yellow* Hawk!" he thundered. "Wouldn't try it alone, would you?"

"Unless you care to surrender, captain," rasped the earphones, "I am afraid I shall never be able to explain my tardiness."

AND AT that moment, a burst of steel smacked through the forward edge of the glass cowl and buried itself in the radio panel.

Dusty's earphones snapped sharply, then went dead. Blind rage gripped him.

He spun around on wing-tip and tore at the nearest Black like a berserk tiger at bay. Whoever the pilot was, he probably never saw Dusty coming. One second the Black ship was curving away, and the next it was plunging straight downward, minus one wing.

But the satisfaction his second victory brought Dusty was short lived. At the beginning of the fight there had been one loophole of escape for him in case he was hemmed in too close. He could always lose himself in the gas curtain and beat a strategic retreat.

But the gaping hole in the forward part of the glass cowl mocked that idea now. Once he entered the gas curtain, the deadly stuff would pour in through that jagged hole and put him out like a light.

His only hope was to fly north to the end of its downward curving crest, and then either skirt the eastern edge or else stake his life on the possibility of the Silver Flash being able to climb over it.

But as he feinted a charge at a zooming Black plane and then cut to the side and around toward the north, his heart sank.

The Blacks must have seen the damage that one of their number had inflicted and calculated the results. For, in half circle formation, they charged in, guns blazing and throwing a wall of whining steel across the northern exit of the area.

The Silver Flash trembled and shivered under the savage hail. It bucked and sawed, and acted as though it were really something alive and conscious of the death ring closing in on it.

A dozen times it went swirling over in a crazy mad spin toward the ground. And a dozen times its cursing master jerked it out and sent it plunging to the north again.

One after another the Blacks smashed in to block the way, and one after another they went skidding out and away from the relentless fire that poured like two continuous streams from Dusty's guns.

How many Blacks he got he did not know. There was no time to watch any balls of fire go hurtling downward. All sense of time became lost to him.

Suddenly, when it seemed that the Silver Flash could hold together no longer, an over-eager Black gave him his one great opportunity. Mad for the kill, the Black came screaming down from the right. Below it was another Black swinging up for a prop-to-prop charge.

THE PURPLE TORNADO

Out of the corner of his eye Dusty saw them, and realization and action became one. With every ounce of his strength he slammed the stick over against the cockpit side. And at the same instant he booted the rudder.

Around he spun, a blur of silver light, then up toward the diving Black. His guns yammered madly and sprayed the diving plane from wing to wing.

Even a blood-maddened Black was not fool enough to hold his position in such a hail of steel. The diving pilot instantly steepened his plunge in a furious effort to slide down under.

And that was a fatal move.

Too late, the Black saw his comrade roaring up. He lurched to the side, but the combined speed of both ships was too great. Their wings locked, a great sheet of flame leaped high up into the canopy of purple gas, and a thunderous roar shook the heavens.

Dusty didn't see them fall. He only saw the hole their finish left in the attacking ring. Like a shot he went through it.

The remaining Blacks tore after him, guns spitting. But Dusty gave the Silver Flash its head. And the plane, like a race horse answering the jockey's whip, leaped forward and out from under the billowing canopy of gas.

"Did it, old girl!" he shouted as he pulled the nose up in a thundering climb toward the east.

But though he had clear air ahead of him, death still rode his wings. Like pack wolves the Blacks came racing after him. And as he tore for the northeastern end of the gas curtain, he suddenly saw a whole squadron of Black attack ships zoom up out of the murky purple.

"Oh yeah!" he laughed harshly. "Still want my hide, eh? Well, just try to stop me!"

Hauling back on the stick, he sent the Silver Flash clawing heavenward. With his free hand he adjusted the oxygen tube to his lips, and turned the valve knob. Now, let them come. Any ship that could out climb the Silver Flash could have a free shot.

But as he muttered the challenge to himself, he suddenly stiffened in the seat. With feverish fingers he turned the valve knob wide open. Then he saw it—saw the jagged bullet hole in the oxygen tank. The burst that had shattered his glass cowl and smashed his radio panel, had also knocked the oxygen tank haywire.

Free fist clenching helplessly, he swept the surrounding skies through narrowed lids. The sight made little fingers of ice clutch at his heart.

Above him was clear air—and suffocation without his oxygen tank. To the front, to the left, and behind was half the Black air force. As though by magic the heavens had suddenly become black with enemy wings.

And to his right was the great towering curtain of deadly gas.

A choice to be made, with death waiting no matter what the choice might be!

In the few moments left before the Blacks would be upon

him again, he battled furiously to make up his mind. Either course he might take was a thousand to one chance for success.

To charge the Blacks that blocked his path to the northeast was but asking for a chest full of singing steel. It was the same thing to his left and behind.

With a grim smile he realized that the Blacks were out to get him. He had penetrated their gas screen, and learned of their offensive preparations. And now, his escape would knock all their efforts into a cocked hat. As a result a general alarm had been sounded along the entire enemy front—get the silver plane! Get it at all costs!

Letting go of the stick for a second, he bent forward, ripped off his tunic and, bundling it into a wad, jammed it into the jagged hole in the glass cowl.

Then skidding the Silver Flash clear of a close burst from one of the Black planes, he heeled sharply over on wing and roared straight into the gas curtain, free hand clamped over his nose and mouth, and breath locked in his lungs!

CHAPTER 4
WANTED FOR MURDER

AN OCEAN of purple swirled about him. Through smarting, slitted eyes he saw it tug and whip at the tunic in the hole.

His face suddenly began to burn, as though he'd plunged it into a seething flame. The joints of his arms and legs went stiff, and the roar of a thousand mighty engines smashed against his eardrums. His lungs ached, and the blood pounded against his temples. But he dared not suck in one tiny drop of air.

The prop wash had jerked free the tunic and with an inward groan he saw it go swirling off into purple space.

Like water gushing through a dam leak, the deadly purple gas poured in through the hole and engulfed him. The skin of his hands and face became raw with pain, and it was impossible to keep his eyes open any longer. Spears of purple flame pierced the eyeballs, and seemed to literally set his brain afire.

Instinctive self-preservation and nothing else forced him to keep one hand clamped over his mouth and nose, and the air in his lungs securely locked. His only comfort was realization that the gas was not of the skin and flesh eroding type. Its first contact with him had proved that.

Each passing second seemed to be the last. He had to breathe—he must gulp in just one small lungful. His chest was ready to explode, and the surging blood in his veins ready to burst through their tissue walls. Yet the fighter in him would not let go. The hand clamped over his nose and mouth seemed almost to melt into it and become a solid part.

Steeling himself against the horrible pain, he opened his eyes a crack and peered ahead. Five times he did that, and saw only a whirling purple vortex in front of him.

And then, when the compressed air in his lungs was forcing itself up his throat, he opened his eyes for the sixth and last time. Through a red blur he saw the dim outlines of trees and hills and valleys below. The ocean of purple was behind him.

Still keeping his hand clamped to his mouth, he let go the

stick and raised the hand up to the cowl-sealing lugs, released them and slammed the cowl wide open. Glorious cool air rushed in at him.

The burning sensation fled and new life surged through his body. Choking, sobbing, and gasping, he gushed out the dead air in his lungs and gulped in blessed coolness. The reaction made his head swim, and a giddy feeling to take charge of his entire body. But he simply relaxed and pumped air into his aching lungs.

Eventually the dizziness passed away, his eyes stopped smarting altogether, and blurred objects came into clear focus. It was then he located his position. He was less than two thousand feet above the pill-box outpost defenses of the U.S. lines. Ahead and several miles to his left was the headquarters of the Z-10 area commander.

Almost unable to realize his good fortune, he turned in the seat and glanced back at the gas curtain. As he did, he saw a flight of Black planes come charging out of it.

"Yup, it's me!" he roared into the propwash rushing past him. "Still on deck, and still going to town!"

Swinging around toward the area H.Q., he stuck the nose down and fed the twenty-eight hundred horses cowled in the nose all the hop they could take.

For a distance of perhaps ten miles the Blacks followed him, and then suddenly they cut sharply away and lost themselves to the west. Dusty curved around, slammed a parting, defiant burst after them, and then throttled and went sliding down toward the area H.Q.

As he landed a hundred yards from the main office, a dozen soldiers ran out and grabbed his wings. One of them, a noncom, saluted him as he legged out stiffly.

"Captain Ayres?" he asked in what seemed to Dusty to be an astonished voice.

"Yes," he nodded.

The noncom swallowed, and fingered his rifle nervously.

"You—you will come with me at once, please, sir," he stammered.

Dusty shot him a sharp look, and glanced at the others. They were watching him as though he were some kind of a freak from another world that had suddenly popped out of the clouds.

"What's the matter with you chaps?" he snapped. "Haven't you ever seen an airplane?"

"Oh, yes, sure, sir!" gulped the noncom. "But, well, we didn't figure on seeing you land here, captain."

Then, as though he had spoken too much, the soldier stiffened and pointed to the main office shack.

"My orders are to take you to General Billings, the area commander, sir. Please come with me."

"That's what I landed for," he grunted. "Let's go. No, wait a minute." He turned to the rest grouped about his plane.

"Get mechanics from the nearest repair depot," he ordered. "I want the radio, the glass cowl and the oxygen tank fixed up as soon as possible."

They blinked at him, then looked at the noncom. Dusty whirled on him, eyes hard.

"Well!" he barked, "what are these men, a lot of dummies? Don't they know an order when they hear one?"

"Our orders were to bring you in, sir," stammered the noncom. "I guess you'll have to speak to General Billings about fixing up your plane, sir."

Dusty hesitated, then nodded.

"Come on, then!" he rapped at the noncom. "Take me to the general."

WITH A look of puzzled surprise still on his face, the noncom kept step with him, ushered him up to the shack door and rapped on it. When a gruff summons to enter came from the inside, he saluted smartly and opened the door.

Dusty went in, clicked his heels, and glared at the big, be-medaled man seated behind the desk.

"You want Captain Ayres, sir?" he snapped.

The general, who was bending over some papers, jerked his head up, started to speak, then let his jaw drop.

"You—Captain Ayres?" he gasped incredulously. "Well, by God, I must say I admire your nerve."

"Nerve had nothing to do with it, sir," Dusty cracked right back at him. "You asked me to do a job for you, and I did it. The Blacks are—"

"Do a job for me?" the commanding officer thundered. "What in hell are you talking about?"

"Talking about?" he echoed slowly. "You remember our radio conversation a couple of hours ago, don't you? You said this place was covered with gas, and that I mustn't land. And later you asked me to reconnoiter back of the gas curtain, well I did, and I want to report that—"

"Wait a minute!"

The general got up from the desk and walked around and over to Dusty.

"Let me have your gun, captain," he said, holding his hand out.

The pilot hesitated, then drew his gun and handed it to the senior officer, butt first. The general took it, half turned to lay it on the desktop then faced Dusty again.

"And now, Captain," he grunted, "just what is this cock-and-bull story you're trying to tell me?"

Dusty gaped at him in angry astonishment.

"You're the Z-10 area commander, aren't you?" he blurted out.

The other nodded his head patiently.

"I am, Captain," he said softly. "As a matter of fact, I have been for the last three weeks."

"Well," frowned Dusty, "two hours ago you asked me to reconnoiter the area back of the Blacks' gas curtain. You said that you believed preparations for an attack were being made."

"Rubbish!" the other cut him off sharply. "The Blacks aren't fools enough to attack at this point. And I certainly didn't ask you any such thing. Frankly, Captain, I just don't understand your landing at my headquarters. Did you think that we hadn't found out yet?"

Dusty's head swam. He stared hard at the senior officer,

struggling for words. They finally came out like a torrent of falling water.

"What in the hell are you talking about?" he demanded.

General Billings didn't answer directly. Instead, he turned and picked up Dusty's gun. Slipping the cartridge magazine out, he examined it closely, slid the loading chamber back and examined that, too. Then he put the muzzle to his nose and sniffed.

"Hum-m!" he mused, arching his eyebrows. "That's rather strange. You certainly didn't use this gun. You have another, Captain?"

"I'm sorry, sir," Dusty grated, "but I still don't know what this is all about. What's my gun got to do with it?"

The general's eyes narrowed, and the muscles about his jaw hardened.

"You have heard of Major Walker, Captain?" he rapped harshly.

Dusty nodded.

"Yes, sir," he said. "I guess he's reported our little meeting. Well, I'm sorry, but considering the circumstances I could not afford to waste any more time convincing him. I told him to contact Washington G.H.Q., but he seemed to believe that I was personally responsible for the death of his cousin, and held a gun on me.

"I didn't feel that it was necessary for me to make detailed explanations to him. I wanted to get a good look at Z-10 area, and then contact your H.Q. I had reason to believe that an attack was to be made here. That much I did tell him. But—well, I hit him. I admit it, sir."

The general's eyes narrowed even more.

"Hit him, eh?" he grunted. "And then shot him?"

Dusty's jaw dropped.

"And then what?" he repeated slowly.

"I said, shot him!" thundered the general. "A patrol found Major Walker shot through the chest.

"He lived long enough to say that a pilot who claimed he was Captain Ayres hit him when he tried to take him to H.Q. for identification, and then shot him. Captain Ayres, Major Walker is dead, and you—on his word—stand accused of murdering him!"

The general paused a moment, and a faint trace of marked disappointment came into his eyes.

"Knowing your records," he went on, "I had hoped that it was someone masquerading as you. A Black agent. A G.H.Q. order for your arrest has been issued. And so, it is my unhappy duty to—"

"Wait!" Dusty shouted. "Do you think if I had killed him I'd be fool enough to land here? I've just damned near lost my neck doing a job for you. Go out and look at my ship. It's all shot to hell. Except for a carload of luck I'd be dead an hour ago."

Some of the hardness went out of the general's eyes.

"You do not need to say anything until your trial, Captain," he said. "But I'd certainly like to hear your side of the story. There was a dead man found with Major Walker. He had been thoroughly searched. For one thing, his right shoe had been taken off, and ripped down the center. Did you do that?"

Dusty hesitated, eyed the general for a moment, then nodded. "Yes, sir. And here's the whole story as far as I know it."

The pilot recounted his experiences from the time of receiving the Black Hawk's challenge right up to the present moment.

"And that, sir," he finished, "is God's truth! It was my intention to turn over that bead and torn paper, you have there, to Washington Intelligence just as soon as I'd reconnoitered the gas curtain area. But circumstances have forced me to tell you everything I know."

A HEAVY silence settled over the room as Dusty stopped. Brows furrowed in puzzled thought, General Billings bent over the green bead and queer diagram Dusty had placed on the desk.

For several moments neither of them spoke. Then the senior officer shot out his right hand and jabbed one of a row of bell buttons that lined the right side of his desk.

A moment later an orderly corporal entered and saluted.

"You rang, sir?"

"Yes, Corporal," nodded the general without looking up. "Ask the radio signal sergeant to report to me at once with today's log."

The orderly saluted and retreated outside. As the door closed, General Billings raised his eyes to Dusty's face.

"A damned queer mess, Captain," he said. "I don't understand it at all. What the devil this bead and crazy diagram can mean, is beyond me. But I want to first check on your conversation with our station. I know nothing of it. And I'll be damned if the signal sergeant issued any such request on his own initiative. We'll see what he has to say, and then contact Washington for further orders."

Dusty nodded absently, and stared hard at the opposite wall. A tiny, elusive thought was spinning around in the back of his brain. Suddenly, he stiffened.

"By God, I wonder!" he breathed fiercely.

General Billings shot him a quizzical glance.

"You wonder what?" he questioned.

Dusty shrugged.

"Don't know just how to put it in words, sir," he got out slowly. "But that bead and the paper—they're dynamite. The man who had them first, this Charles Strickland, died before he could explain. Later, Major Walker died. In the meantime—"

He suddenly stopped.

"By God, I think I've got it!" he continued a few seconds later. "I'll bet I didn't talk with this station at all. I'll bet the Blacks cut in on my wave-length, blanketed out my signals to you, and lured me over to their side of the lines for a killing. They did every damned thing possible to prevent my returning. Because I'd seen their preparations for an attack? Hell, no. Because they were afraid that Strickland had told me something.

"Yes, sir, that bead and that paper mean something damned big, or else I'm crazy. They've killed, or tried to kill, everyone who has been near it. Maybe I may annoy the Blacks every now and then, but they've never sent a couple of hundred ships after me yet! And the Hawk failed to meet me as arranged. Sure,

Strickland was a Yank agent. He got hold of something important and tried to get through to the American side."

In silence General Billings drummed his fingers on the desk.

"There are still a few holes to be filled in," he murmured. "According to you, Major Walker claimed that Strickland was refused enlistment, and didn't know how to fly. Incidentally, your telling me that is a point in your favor. I mean, the very fact that you told something that could be used against you at the trial."

"Good God, do you still think—?"

"It's not for me to make a final decision, Captain," the other cut him off. "That's up to a military court. My orders are simply to place you under arrest, if I find you. At your trial you can—"

"Trial, hell!" Dusty exploded. "That may not be for weeks. And in the meantime, there's plenty for me to do."

"Do what, Captain?"

The pilot leaned over the desk, his eyes were agate and the hands gripping the edge were white at the knuckles.

"Find out the answer to that bead and paper!" he got out through tight lips. "I know where the answer is, and I'm the one who can get it!"

The general arched his eyebrows.

"Really!" he murmured patiently. "And just where is the answer, Captain?"

"The Black Hawk has the answer. And I'll hammer it out of him with my two hands, if it's the last thing I do!"

The general seemed unimpressed by the savage outburst.

"Perhaps, captain," he smiled. "From all I've heard of you I'm sure you'll tackle any kind of a task. But it so happens that the matter is not entirely in your hands. For the moment, the murder of a distinguished artillery officer is the paramount item."

"But the Black Hawk!" cut in Dusty excitedly. "He—!"

"Has only to do with your deductions, Captain!" General Billings snapped. "Just whether this bead and paper mean anything, remains to be seen. If Strickland said that an attack was planned in this area, he was certainly mistaken. The Blacks know of our defenses, and realize that any attempt could not possibly move with success. So we need not worry about that."

Dusty gritted his teeth and groaned.

"Then I'm *non compos mentis* until a military court gets around to deciding one way or the other, is that it?"

The senior officer hunched his shoulders, and nodded.

"That's about it. I'm sorry, Captain. Section fourteen, paragraph twelve of the revised Army Rules and Regulations will tell you that a soldier or officer charged with a major offense cannot be reinstated to active duty until the charges against him are dismissed by a governing military court."

"But I tell you—"

Dusty bit off the rest as the general raised a silencing hand. Burning with rage, he walked over and glared blindly out the window. Silence, heavy and tense, again settled over the room.

And then the door burst open and the orderly corporal came panting inside. His eyes were wide, and he fought for breath a few seconds before he was able to get the words out.

"Sir!" he choked. "Sergeant Crabtree—the radio sergeant! He's been murdered, shot through the heart. In the radio shack!"

General Billings knocked over the chair as he leaped to his feet.

"What?" he thundered.

The orderly bobbed his head up and down.

"Y-Yes, sir!" he gulped out. "Sergeant Crabtree's been shot through the heart. And all the radio equipment has been smashed to hell—to pieces, sir!"

CHAPTER 5
DEATH DROME

IT SEEMED to take General Billings several seconds to grasp the full meaning of the orderly's words. Dusty, who had spun around from the window at the sudden entrance, stood poised on the balls of his feet, eyes glued to the general's face.

Suddenly the senior officer started toward the door.

"Come along, Corporal," he snapped. "Show me!"

Why he did it Dusty couldn't explain to himself at the moment, but, as the general started through the door, he shot out a hand, scooped up his automatic, the green bead and the torn diagram, and jammed them all in his breeches pocket. Then spinning around, he raced out of the office and after the others.

The radio shack was a good two hundred yards from the main area office, and all three men were panting hard when they reached the door. General Billings entered first, with Dusty and the orderly corporal at his heels.

The interior of the place looked as though an H.E. battery had scored a direct salvo hit. Every piece of equipment from the delicate transmitting and receiving tubes to the heavy rubber batteries had been smashed beyond all hope of repair. So much so, in fact, Dusty realized instantly that an entirely new station would have to be installed.

But the thing that caught and held the eyes of all three was the limp figure sprawled face up on the steel and copper floor just under the speaker units.

He wore the uniform of a radio signal sergeant, and was probably no more than twenty, if that. The eyes were open and in their death-glazed depths there was a glint of horrified surprise. The out-flung hands were doubled into hard fists, and one leg was twisted under him. The part of the man's fatigue tunic that covered the heart region was stained a dull, glistening red.

"Good God!" gulped General Billings, as he stood staring down at the still figure. "It's—it's impossible!"

Brushing past him, Dusty knelt down and opened the man's tunic front and shirt. Just a shade to the left of the breast bone was an ugly quarter-inch hole that was oozing sluggish blood.

Controlling the shudder the sight sent through him, he pulled the man's tunic together and stood up.

"I'm afraid that you'll have to believe it, sir," he said quietly, facing the general. "He got it right through the heart. I'd say a regulation Army .45 was used. Not so long ago, either!"

The pilot's words seemed to rouse the general from his stupor. He let his eyes rove about the room.

"Every blasted thing's smashed!" he grunted angrily. "Have to replace it all. But why?"

"I think that someone wanted to make sure you couldn't contact any other units," replied Dusty. And then as an after-thought, "Particularly Washington H.Q."

The general stared at him.

"You mean, because of that crazy theory of yours?" he demanded.

Dusty silenced him with a warning glance.

"Yes, sir," he said simply. "Because of my theory. I connect up the three deaths with it. This last, just as a precautionary measure. A Black agent right here at your H.Q. did this job, and then contacted one of his own stations!"

The senior officer snorted.

"How the devil do you figure out that, Captain?"

Dusty stepped over the dead man and pointed at the in-coming and out-going message recorder. It was shaped something like a stock ticker tape machine, only now the glass dome was broken and the delicate gears and cog-checks mashed hopelessly out of line.

"See this, sir?" he said, taping a strip of the tap. "Voice transmission hasn't been recorded for the last four hours. That means that my call signals were not picked up. The Blacks blanketed them out. But see here—this torn piece? It recorded dot-dash signals sent out less than an hour ago."

General Billings came over and peered hard at the dangling ribbon of tape covered with dot and dash marks.

"Well, what about it?" he got out gruffly. "We use wireless as well as radio. I often send out orders in coded Morse."

"Quite right, sir," nodded Dusty patiently. "But this is not International Morse! Take this one symbol here—two dots, two dashes and three dots. There isn't a signal letter or figure like that in International Morse. Now I can't say for sure, but I think this is part of a message sent out in the secret speed code that the Blacks developed in Europe."

The pilot suddenly stopped talking, went quickly across the debris-littered room and picked up a massive radio log lying on top of a table. Spinning the pages to the last entry, he studied it a long second, and nodded his head.

"Looks like I'm right," he said holding up the log. "The last entry was made at ten fifty-six—a request for miscellaneous stores for the 20th infantry, this area. But there's no entry for those code signals on the tape."

AS THOUGH reluctant to believe him, General Billings went over to Dusty, practically snatched the radio log from his hands and glared at it, brows furrowed. Presently he slapped the log shut and tossed it on the desk.

"By God, I still can't believe it!" he growled with a stubborn movement of his lower lip. "A Black agent in my headquarters? Bah! It's probably someone who had a grudge against Sergeant Crabtree."

"And a grudge against all this expensive equipment too, sir?" murmured Dusty.

The other whirled on him angrily.

"See here, Ayres!" he barked, "you're forgetting that you're—"

"No, I'm not!" Dusty cracked down on him. "I'm only asking you to believe that I did see the signs of a big Black offensive against this area! What happens to me, is out of it. I'm only asking you to let me carry on with the job of trying to unravel this mess. It's big, General—something damned big. The very fact that the Blacks are preparing for a mighty blow at this sector proves that there's something else behind it. As you say they're no fools. They're not going to bang their heads against a steel wall, and just pray. That dia—"

Dusty cut himself off as out the corner of his eye he saw the orderly sliding toward the door. He swung around in a flash and took a step forward.

"You! Where are you going?"

As he spoke, his foot caught on the table leg and he stumbled to his knees. Instantly something glittered in the orderly's hand. A white-hot bullet slid across Dusty's left shoulder. Behind him a sharp cry rang out.

One hand and knee still on the floor, he jerked his automatic free, swung it up and fired at a blur in the doorway. The blur disappeared and he saw the gouge mark his bullet made in the metal jamb.

Hurtling to his feet he leaped forward, flung himself through and down onto the ground. There was a sharp *crack* and dirt flew up into his eyes. As he rolled furiously to the left he saw the orderly, crouched behind a field phone pole, steady himself and take careful aim. Still in motion, Dusty threw out his gun hand and pulled the trigger.

The two shots were so close together that they seemed like

THE PURPLE TORNADO

53

one. Something stung Dusty's hand and sent his gun flying. As he cursed and grabbed for it, he saw the orderly collapse on his back. A wild scream beat against the air.

Scooping up his gun with numbed fingers, he raced over to him and bent down. A second shot was not necessary. There was a small blue hole square between the man's close set eyes.

Looking down at the face, Dusty noticed, with a glow of satisfaction, something that he had not seen before. The features, save for the lightness of the skin—possible to obtain with certain chemicals—were distinctly cruel-looking and hawkish in appearance.

"You tried to work too fast!" he grated softly. "A nice bit of acting, all the excited stuff—but when you heard me guessing things that clicked, you got just a bit nervous."

By now the whole H.Q. was in an uproar. Soldiers and officers of all ranks came pouring out of the buildings. In a matter of seconds there was a mob gathered about Dusty. As he started to shoulder his way through, a staff Major grabbed him.

Dusty shook himself free.

"Get a medico!" he snapped. "That spy just missed me and got General Billings. I think the general is hurt."

Without waiting for any more questions, he put his head down, plowed through the ring of officers and soldiers and ran back to the radio building. The others followed.

Slumped down on the floor, legs crossed under him, General Billings was clutching blood-smeared fingers to his stomach, and bracing himself against the desk with his other hand.

"A medico's coming, sir," said Dusty gently as he crouched down beside the moaning man. "Better lay down, sir."

"Damned—if you—weren't right, Captain. It's four—killings now. Meant for you—but you—tripped. Lucky, lad. Did—did you—?"

"Don't try to talk," cautioned Dusty. "Yes, I got him. He's dead. He meant to get us both, I think. Probably heard us talking in your office. Now take it easy, sir."

The general glared, and coughed blood.

"Hell, know when I'm done! Major Shelton, Shelton—damn, do you hear me?"

The staff major who had grabbed Dusty stepped quickly forward and kneeled down.

"Yes, sir? What can I do for you, General?"

The wounded man let go of the desk long enough to point a finger at Dusty.

"This officer is—Captain Ayres," he choked out. "My orders—give him all—the cooperation—he wants. Understand?"

The major shot Dusty a piercing look.

"Yes, sir," he said to General Billings. "Certainly!"

The fast-graying lips of the senior officer twitched back in a faint smile as he turned his head to Dusty.

"Believe you, now—Captain," he gurgled. "You must be right. I'm—giving you your freedom on—your word! Find out—your way. And give them—hell—for me! Will you, Ca—cap—?"
THE LAST was too much for the man. His eyes went wide, and blood sprayed from his lips. Then he seemed to catch his breath in a wheezing gasp and slumped forward.

55

"One side, gentlemen! One side please!"

A short mustached medico came shouldering through the mob that had crowded into the radio shack. But he stopped short as he saw the look on Dusty's face.

"I think so," said Dusty, shaking his head. "Better make sure, though."

It took the medico about twenty seconds to do that.

"He's gone," he said quietly. "Internal hemorrhage, and a rib deflected the bullet to the spine. How'd it happen? I saw a dead orderly lying near the pole outside."

In as few words as possible Dusty told of the double killing, but did not mention any of the events that had passed before.

When he finished they all stood looking at him with speculative eyes. It was the staff major who finally put the question uppermost in every mind.

"Just a minute, Captain Ayres," he began hesitantly. "If you don't mind we'd like to hear more of the facts. Of course we know of your little er—affair. And although General Billings ordered me to—"

He stopped short as Dusty shook his head.

"You mean you won't tell us, Captain?" he got out harshly.

"I'm afraid I do, sir," said Dusty slowly. "But I will say this much. The enemy is planning an attack against this area, although I have reason to believe that it will not be launched as long as I'm alive. So far, four Americans and one Black agent have died because of a certain scrap of paper. Knowledge of the contents of that paper means death. No, I'm not trying to be dramatic—"

Dusty hesitated, and gave Major Shelton an appraising glance.

"May I speak with you alone, outside?" he asked suddenly.

The other nodded, turned on his heel, and shouldered his way through the crowd. Once he was out of earshot of the group in the radio building, he turned and fixed Dusty with steady eyes.

"Well, what's it all about?" he snapped.

The pilot gave him look for look.

"I want you to carry out General Billing's last order, Major," he said. "How far is the nearest radio station from here?"

"Second infantry, twenty miles east of here. Why?"

Dusty spoke slowly, carefully choosing his words.

"I want you to call the Second Infantry," he said. "Explain to them that your station was wrecked, and tell them to notify Washington H.Q. that your radio operator, a Black agent, General Billings and myself have been killed. Say that the reason for the deaths is not known, and that you are awaiting further orders."

The staff major stared at him as though he had suddenly gone crazy.

"That you were killed?" he echoed. "What the devils the idea?"

Dusty grinned.

"Just part of a little plan," he said. "I'm sorry, but I'd rather keep it to myself. If I flop, there'll be no come-back on you, I assure you."

Major Shelton scowled at the ground, and marked a crazy pattern in the dirt with the toe of one shoe. Presently he muttered a curse of annoyance under his breath, and jerked his head up.

"I know of your special appointment, Captain," he said evenly. "And of the G.H.Q. request that assistance be given you when demanded. But I consider that the general order for your arrest has changed that somewhat. Incidentally, this does not happen to be a one-man war. I think, instead that I'll notify Washington H.Q. of what has happened and ask for orders from them direct."

"If you do, Major," Dusty grated at him, "you may be signing your own death warrant."

The other arched, gave Dusty a contemptuous look.

"I guess I can chance that," he said lightly.

For a minute or so they both stood there, eyes locked and bodies tensed. It was Dusty who eventually broke the spell.

"Believe me, Major," he said earnestly, "I know what I'm talking about. The broadcast of my death will sure to be picked up by the Blacks. It will give me the chance to carry out the rest of my plan. I ask you as one American soldier to another, please carry out my request. It—hell, it may mean everything!"

Perhaps it was the sincerity in Dusty's tone, or the grim anxiety on his face. But, at any rate, after a moment's pause, Major Shelton smiled slowly and nodded his head.

"All right," he said quietly. "This is the first time in sixteen years of army life that a junior officer has talked me into going against my better judgment. I'll do as you ask."

In spite of himself, Dusty heaved a great sigh of relief.

"Thanks, sir! Now, one more favor. About my ship—it needs repairs, and—"

"I know," the other cut in. "One of the men said you ordered repairs. We have the necessary parts here. We carry the stuff for staff ships."

Dusty beamed.

"Swell," he exclaimed. "That's what I call luck. Get the men at it right away, will you, sir? Won't take them more than an hour. And I'll be ready then."

"All right," shrugged Major Shelton. "But I certainly wish that you'd tell—oh, let it go. Guess I always did have a soft spot for crazy Indians."

The staff officer turned on his heel and walked away. Dusty smiled at his back a moment, and then looked toward the gas curtain still hanging in the northern heavens. The smile faded from his lips; jaw muscles tightened, and his hands slowly doubled into steel knotted fists.

"Now, you dirty skunks!" he gritted out between clenched teeth, "it's my turn to deal a hand!"

He walked quickly over to the area H.Q. shack and shouldered inside.

CHAPTER 6
THE HANGING DOOM

CHIN PROPPED in his hands, elbows propped on the edge of the desk, Dusty stared silently down at the torn diagram. For over half an hour he had not taken his eyes off the paper. Its meaning, if any, still eluded him. But that was not the purpose uppermost in his mind. He had been slowly and methodically memorizing the strange diagram until at last every crease, every line, and every figure was stamped indelibly upon his brain.

Presently he leaned back, blinked his tired eyes, then dropped the torn sheet into an ash tray and applied a match. A minute later it was a crinkled, charred strip that became so much black dust under his tamping finger.

"Just in case Lady Luck gives me the go-by," he grunted, and spilled the dust into the wastepaper basket.

Picking up the green bead, he scowled thoughtfully at it a moment then jammed it into the seam of his right breeches pocket. Hardly had he finished that, than a noise outside the door made him stiffen and shoot out a hand for his automatic close by on the desk. Its muzzle was trained dead on the door as it opened.

At the sight of Major Shelton's head he relaxed and lowered the gun.

"Your plane's ready, Ayres," grunted the staff officer, eyes riveted on the gun. "What's next?"

"The next is up to me, sir," he said. "But I want to thank you for everything."

"Cut it!" snapped the other. "I'm half inclined to change my mind. God knows I'll be in a pretty pickle when Washington H.Q. starts checking back on everything. Sure you want to play this mysterious plan of yours alone?"

The pilot nodded his head firmly.

"Dead sure," he said shortly. "You've equipment here for smoke screening enemy air raiders, haven't you?"

"That's right," Major Shelton clipped out. "Good God, that, too?"

Dusty gestured.

"Naturally, sir! I can't take off in broad daylight, and simply hope that enemy pilots on patrol will look the other way. A smoke screen will cover me perfectly. I can be in the cloud layer before it fades out. And any Blacks that see the screen will just think that this H.Q. has got the wind-up over a possible raid."

"You think of everything, don't you?" the other snorted. "Very well, I'll give you your smoke screen. But listen, young fellow. If I do get into hot water, I'm going to raise heaven and hell to pull you in with me. That's a warning."

"Check, sir," grinned Dusty. "And thank—"

"Shut up! and good luck on whatever the hell's in that head of yours."

Darting through the door, the staff officer slammed it shut. Five minutes later Dusty followed him outside.

It was like stepping out into a swirling sand storm, minus the sand. At first he could see nothing. Great waves of oily gray smoke swished and swirled about him. Buildings less than fifty yards away looked like dull blotches in a heavy rolling gray mist. Beyond them nothing was visible.

Pausing a second to get his bearings, he turned half right and plunged into the billowing shroud.

He stopped only when he almost ran into the Silver Flash, and a shadowy figure grabbed him.

"Right here, Ayres," sounded Major Shelton's sharp voice in his ears. "Hope its thick enough for you. In case you're wondering, you've got a clear run of about a hundred yards straight in front of you. The top of this stuff should reach fifteen thousand. That okay?"

"Couldn't be better," Dusty called over his shoulder, as he legged into the pit. "Give me two minutes, and then you can shut the stuff off."

As an after-thought, just before he slid the cowling closed, he called back.

"And send the laundry bill to me, Major!"

"Don't worry, I will!" echoed back to him. "The damned stuff, it—"

The rest was lost to Dusty as he heeled open the throttle and released the wheel brakes.

As though eager to get into the air again, the Silver Flash leaped forward, clung to the ground for a bare twenty yards, and then went zooming up blindly into the smoke screen.

Holding the nose up and to the south, Dusty gave the ship all it could take, and swept the cockpit's fittings with a practiced eye.

Everything was as it should be. New glass replaced the shattered strip, a new radio panel adorned the dash board, and a replacement oxygen tank was clamped to the cockpit side. The rest of the instruments, including the guns, had been checked and put in perfect working order.

Dusty grinned and snapped one hand up in congratulatory salute.

"Nice work, lads," he grunted aloud. "I'll remember you next time something goes wrong."

THE INSPECTION over with, and everything found to be okay, his face went grave and a look of half anxiousness and half savage determination came into his eyes.

Up to now a definite plan had been crystallized in his mind. And it all revolved about the Black Hawk. That sky vulture knew the answers to all the questions which baffled him, he believed beyond all possible doubt.

Next to Fire-Eyes, himself, in importance, the Hawk undoubtedly knew every major plan of the Black Invaders. And a major plan was slowly but surely coming to a head—to a thundering, roaring climax.

But the nature of that plan the Yank did not know. He was only certain that there was some great scheme about to be sprung by the Blacks. Call it a hunch, or premonition, or just plain guess work, it didn't matter which. Past events hooked up too closely to be put down to coincidence.

"Damn it, there must be!" he argued aloud to himself. "And that torn diagram is the key. Strickland, Walker, the radio sergeant, and General Billings—all killed because of it. And they tried their damnedest to get me. God, if I could only figure it out!"

He stopped talking long enough to smash a clenched fist against the cockpit side.

"But you, Black Hawk!" he blazed. "You're going to tell me about it, even if I have to break your damned—"

As a heart chilling thought came to him, he cut off the rest. Was the Hawk still alive? Had the Hawk been in one of those Black ships he'd sent hurtling downward a couple of hours ago?

The sudden thought deadened the fire of determination that burned in his chest. He'd shot off his face to General Billings, vowed that he'd get the answers from the Hawk—and had pleaded for the chance.

Well, murder had given him that chance. Now, he was in the air to hunt down the Black ace—but was he still alive? For a moment the bottom seemed to drop out of everything. The small quiet voice inside of him called him a fool and flayed his confidence for its assumed belief that he alone could succeed in following the tiny strands of the spidery web to the center, and disrupt the whole thing.

Certainly he was a crazy fool. He should have reported to Washington H.Q. hours ago. If he had, these other murders probably never would have happened.

If the bead and the torn diagram meant anything it was up to Intelligence to figure it out, not an over-zealous eagle like himself.

He reached out his free hand to the wave-length knob to notify Washington H.Q. that he was coming in to report.

Then with a savage curse he jerked back.

"Like hell I will!" he roared out. "I started this, and I'll finish it. If the Hawk's dead, I'll get the answers some other way!"

As the last ripped off his lips, the nose of the Silver Flash poked itself up through the top of the smoke screen. Leveling off, Dusty hugged close to its crest and searched the surrounding air through narrowed lids.

Between him and the cloud layer was a space a bit less than a thousand feet deep. Half a minute was all he needed to bury himself in the cloud layer. But first, before roaring up into the thousand-foot channel of clear air, he had to make sure that no patrolling Black planes were about.

One sweeping look east, south and west resulted in nothing but clear air, not even a tiny dot in the distance. But as he looked north, toward the gas curtain, he stiffened in his seat. A flight of Black ships was weaving in and out of the billowing mass.

But a few moments later, he gave a shout of joy and jerked the nose of the Silver Flash upward. As though tired of their fruitless patrol all of the Black planes had suddenly plunged into the gas curtain and become lost to view.

Eyes glued to the spot where they had disappeared, Dusty cursed his own ship on to greater speed. And when at last the misty tentacles of the cloud layer gathered him into their blind depths, his heart was looping over with triumphant relief.

So far, so good. He had gained his first objective. Now to fly compass in the cloud layer to a point far behind the Black defenses.

Swinging around to the northwest, he glued his eye to the instrument board and sent the Silver Flash charging forward.

Little tingles of excitement and worry rippled up and down his spine. Flying blind didn't bother him in the least. He'd had too much experience in that phase of the game. Besides, his instruments never lied.

But still and all there was one danger that might be lurking near at hand—a danger that he might be forced to meet and overcome in the bat of an eyelash. And that danger was the possibility of a collision with some enemy plane drifting about in the cloud layer.

But as he toyed with the thought, he shrugged. It was a chance that had to be taken—and that was all there was to it. A FEW moments later, though, a black shadow came rushing through the cloud layer toward him. His heart stood still, and he started to hurl the Silver Flash off to the right and up. Almost instantly he checked the movement, and a shaky laugh spilled off his lips. He was simply flying through the section where the gas curtain passed up through the cloud layer.

Instinctively he glanced up to make sure that the cowl-sealing lugs were locked in place. They were. He ruddered the ship back onto its original course. Seconds ticked by and became minutes—five of them, ten—fifteen—

Gr-r-rump!

Sound, like the heavy bark of a mighty Saint Bernard, came to him through the cowling. Off to the left a dull ball of flame appeared in the cloud layer, hung motionless for an instant, and then fused out.

Hardly had it disappeared than there was sound and flame off to the right. Groaning with rage, he banked and deliberately flew toward it.

Seconds later he zigzagged sharply back in the opposite direction. Behind him he heard a third explosion.

"Dummy!" he blazed at himself as he savagely zigzagged this way and that. "Did you think the Blacks would leave their sound detectors home?"

Blindly cursing his own stupidity for not having taken the

very natural existence of enemy sound detectors and amplifiers into consideration, he slowly eased the Silver Flash up toward the top of the cloud layers.

About him, in the shroud mist, shells were spewing out their balls of fused red fire, "bracketing" his ever-changing position, and warning patrolling pilots of the presence of an enemy airplane.

To go down, now, was out of the question. For the moment at least, his wild plan was knocked into a cocked hat. His only hope lay in climbing up to peak ceiling, cutting his engine and gliding down to a point at least a hundred miles north of the Black lines.

Then, at half throttle, and keeping just inside the cloud layer, he could drift back and pick out a spot to land in close by the Hawk's drome.

That he'd find it he had no doubt. Only the Hawk's unit flew the speedy arrow-shaped Dart monoplanes. And once he found their nest, there would he find the man he sought—or would he?

He cursed the question out of his mind. Time to worry about that later. Right now it was up to the Silver Flash to claw air upward and claw it fast. The Blacks knew that an enemy plane was hidden in the cloud layer, but they didn't know the identify of the pilot.

A minute later he roared into clear air—less than two thousand feet above him was a whole unit of Black attack planes. And in a split second it took to whip the Silver Flash down into the cloud layer again he caught a glimpse to the south of an enemy bomber flight lumbering toward his position in strung-out line position.

Had he more time he would have noticed something else. As it was, with a gasping sigh of relief, he buried himself in the cloud layer, totally unaware of the shroud of doom that was relentlessly closing in on him.

CHAPTER 7
SILVER FIRE

KEEPING THE Sliver Flash throttled all the way back, he held it in a shallow glide toward the northwest. With escape by altitude lost, he could only stake his hopes on being able to stay in the cloud layer long enough to get out of range of the sound detectors.

But as the seconds ticked by and the airspeed indicator needle hovered dangerously close to the stalling mark, his heart sank. Bitter desperation seized him. It was either down or up for him now. To open up would be but a waste of time. He was still within the range of the detectors, and already the gunners were poking around for his new position.

"All right, miracle man!" he groaned sadly. "This washes up your pet plan! So take a look-see and get the hell back to your own side of the fence."

Oblivious to the pain that shot through his hand, he banged the throttle wide open, and stuck the nose down.

The sudden, furious thunder of the roaring twenty-eight hundred horses cowled into the nose deafened him for an instant. But a few seconds later as he shot down into clear air, he forgot all about his vibrating eardrums.

Below him on the ground was a scene that sent his heart pounding with excitement. The earth seemed to be virtually covered with countless streamlined tractor troop trains, tank units, and armored field guns on tread-trucks.

But it was not the sight of them that startled him, so much as it was the fact that they were all crawling along behind the gas curtain in a southwesterly direction. In fact they were just inside the northern lip of the downward curving curtain.

Without taking the trouble to glance at his roller map for confirmation, Dusty realized instantly that the gigantic caravan of war was at least one hundred fifty miles behind the Black's main defenses—and headed southwest, away from the Z-10 area!

Yet, as he thundered through the back flap of the curving gas curtain and into the clear again, he saw far to the southeast the same panorama of offensive warfare that he'd seen a few hours before.

A mighty army, guns, tanks and everything else, was converging on the frontier of the Z-10 area. Yet one hundred fifty miles behind it, an even greater steel clad horde was moving slowly southwest along the northern borders of New Hampshire and Vermont.

Two great sledge hammers of war, one moving southeast and the other southwest. And shielding both movements from the American side of the line was a towering curtain of thick, heavy and deadly gas.

Wide-eyed, Dusty stared at the weird yet blood-chilling sight. He was certain that a great offensive would soon be launched against the Z-10 area. This second view of the obvious preparation was just so much confirmation.

But that second and even greater army crawling southwest was like a big question mark burning in his brain.

Could the Blacks be planning offensives at two points? If so, what was the other point? To the southwest lay the Great Lakes, Yanks on one side and Blacks on the other, and miles and miles of vigilantly patrolled waters between them.

And then, like a spear of light, a thought flashed through Dusty's spinning brain. It jerked him up straight in the seat.

"My God!" he exclaimed. "Is that it?"

Trembling with excitement, he ignored the shells that started barking in his wake, snapped out his hand and spun the wavelength dial.

"Emergency, Washington H.Q.!" he bellowed into the transmitter, turning up full volume. "Emergency… stand by!"

Breathlessly he glued his eyes to the red signal light on the panel and strained his ears for the familiar crackle in the phones. One second, two seconds… three.

His body went clammy with eerie dread, and sweat oozed out on his forehead and trickled off in drops.

"Washington H.Q., emergency!" he called again. "Emergency… emergency. Captain Ayres calling Washington H.Q."

A split second later the signal light blinked, and the phones hummed.

"Go ahead, Captain Ayres. What would you like to tell your commanders?"

A harsh laugh followed the rasping words. Dusty sat rigid as the hated voice of the Black Hawk continued.

"Did you suppose your little death broadcast and smoke screen trick would blind us? Did you think we have only *one* secret agent working for us…?"

Dusty was no longer listening. He was searching the air for a glimpse of a sleek jet-black monoplane. But there was none to be seen. Subconsciously, he realized that the gunners below had stopped firing at him.

"—and, I might add, Captain, that the staff major has now joined that very stupid General Billings. So that leaves only you."

"Damn it!" Dusty blurted out. "Show yourself, and I'll do the rest!"

The chuckle in the earphones mocked him.

"Bravo, Captain! My compliments on your courage. But my fancy holds me in check, at the moment."

Dusty began hurling his ship around in mad, questing circles. But though he searched until his eyeballs ached, not one single sign of a Black ship did he see. And all the time the rasping voice of the Black Hawk maintained a taunting chatter in the earphones.

SUDDENLY HE swung the Silver Flash toward the south, fed the engine all the hop it could take.

"Some other time!" he howled into the transmitter. "I've got other things to do right now."

Easing the nose down a bit, he waited expectantly for the Hawk to stop his hide-and-seek game and come plunging down out of the cloud layer to give battle.

But as the seconds whipped by, even that hope vanished. Wherever he was, the Black pilot seemed bent on remaining there.

And then, suddenly, there was a sound like the booming of a naval gun in the Yanks earphones.

He jumped violently in spite of himself, and the Silver Flash skidded crazily off to the side under the sudden and uncontrollable jerk of his hand.

Ears ringing, he checked the wild movement of the plane, hauled it back onto even keel, and sent it screaming up toward the cloud layer.

An instinctive warning had shot through his body. The Hawk was not playing this game of hide-and-seek for nothing. And it was plumb foolishness to wait down in clear air for the Black to finally show himself.

In the back of his brain he was putting the pieces of the puzzle together bit by bit. And although the picture was not entirely clear as yet, he had more than enough to work on. In fact, enough to cause his heart to pound furiously against his ribs and cold sweat to splash off his forehead.

Outlined in fire against the screen of memory in his head was the torn diagram he had taken from Strickland. The more he studied it with his mind's eye the more clear it became.

Gone was the mystery that had surrounded it a few hours ago. He knew now—knew the truth! And realization set the blood in his veins to boiling, and fired him with a determination to get through to the American lines before it was too late.

He pounded his free fist against the throttle.

"Come on, old girl, get going!" he yelled hoarsely. "We've got to make it. Got to make it now!"

And then suddenly it happened—happened so quickly that his brain was unable to scream an order to his hands before it was too late.

Right in front of him, a curtain of dangling cable wires shot down out of the cloud layer.

Like so many thin, gray snakes they twisted and screwed about in the air. A wild cry of alarm clogged in his throat as he frantically belted the stick over against the cockpit side, and slammed all his weight on the rudder pedal.

The Silver Flash seemed to groan aloud as it tried to respond instantly to the vicious movement of the controls. It lurched off to the side, seemed to hover motionless as its prop clawed madly.

And then it plunged downward.

But too late.

The terrific forward speed of the plane was too great, and the curtain of dangling gray wires too close.

In the split second left him, Dusty saw the network of connecting strands that held the vertical cable wires in place— saw the interlocking mesh barrier come sweeping toward him.

And then, helpless to do anything, he went plowing right into it.

As though made of rubber instead of fine cable wire, the sky net seemed to give way to the force of the impact. But only for a matter of split seconds, and then the cables went taut, and Dusty was flung up against the instrument board with crushing force.

Half conscious, he reeled back into the seat.

Through blurred eyes he saw his prop clashing and ripping at the maze of twisting and whipping cable wires. They snapped with the report of pistol shots, but their loose ends slapped back and wound themselves about the prop shaft.

Others curled back over the wings and gouged long grooves in the metal covering.

And yet, as though it were something human—like a Bengal tiger caught in the hunters' stout rope net—the Silver Flash bucked and yawned and strained mightily, to break through the countless thin, gray fingers that curled themselves about it from prop to tailskid.

And slamming the stick about, and sawing rudder, Dusty added every bit of his flying skill in a mad effort to help the plane break through.

But it was useless.

The sky net wound its steel fingers about the shaft of the thrashing propeller. Presently, the engine sputtered, broke itself free for an instant with a mighty roar, and then sputtered and backfired some more.

Black smoke spewed out from its exhaust vents and smeared great streaks of soot oil along the glass cowling. Vibration shook the plane like a leaf in a tornado, and a second later one of the

THE PURPLE TORNADO

AND THEN, HELPLESS TO DO ANYTHING, HE WENT PLOWING RIGHT INTO IT.

75

wing internal bracing wires let go with a singing *twang* that echoed against Dusty's eardrums like the bells of doom.

One eye blinded by the blood that flowed down from an ugly gash on his forehead, Dusty somehow managed to haul back the throttle and snap off the ignition switch.

Its power gone, the prop snapped to an instant stop. And then, as though unable to hold out any longer, the variable pitch gears flew off in pieces, and the blades of the prop itself followed them into oblivion a moment later.

Dully conscious that he was still able to work the controls after a fashion, Dusty virtually lifted the ship over on one wing, slammed on top rudder and let the tail swing down to the vertical.

It was his only hope—and it worked. The mesh curtain, that had immediately been released from above at the moment of impact, went swishing forward and jerked the remainder of its dangling strands free from the nose of the plane.

But it had already done its work and the fact that its twisted and tangled remains dropped clear of him brought no sense of joy to Dusty's heart.

He was through—and in due time the Silver Flash II would be no more.

As his mind rushed backward and he remembered those bombers in strung-out line formation, he groaned aloud in bitter agony.

Like mine sweepers sweeping their great steel nets through the waters, those Black bombers had swept the skies. And watchers on the ground had signaled when to let the nets out to their full length. That signal had been the booming sound in the earphones.

HALF MAD with blind rage, Dusty jerked the plane out of its lumbering dive and stared at the ground below. There, less than five miles to the west, was an enemy airdrome, and in front of its row of hangars a long line of Black Dart monoplanes. The Black Hawk's drome—the objective of his crazy plan!

Plan? He laughed harshly. Plan, hell. What plan did he have? He, a helpless eagle floating down to a hit-or-miss landing in enemy country—and a million pairs of eyes watching him.

"To the west, Captain. You are to land on my field. And after we land you can thank me for saving your life."

The crackling voice of the Black Hawk in the earphones startled Dusty. Snapping his head back, he saw a Black bomber slide down out of the cloud layer.

From snap-releases fitted to the spar ends of both lower wings, shreds of the sky net flapped backward in the prop wash. Though he could not see the figure in the pilots' compartments, Dusty knew instinctively that the Hawk was there. Too yellow to risk his precious neck, the man had hidden in the clouds until his trap had been sprung.

Like a beam of brilliant light cutting through impenetrable darkness, the last words of the Hawk touched a note of sudden realization in his brain. The Hawk wanted him alive, yet a few hours ago they had moved heaven and hell in a desperate effort to kill him.

Why? As Dusty told himself the answer, his lips curled back in a hard smile.

"You're worried," he murmured softly, "and you want to make sure. Well stew in your own juice a while!"

And then in loud tones.

"Hey tramp! Signal down to clear your field. My ship won't hold out much longer and I'll have to land fast!"

The ear-phones chuckled.

"Unfortunate, isn't it captain? Very well, I'll signal to them. Land at the north end. And be careful, captain. Should you—"

Dusty didn't hear the rest. With a flick of his free hand he cut off the radio. At the same time he stuck the nose of the propless Silver Flash straight downward.

The damaged wings shook dangerously, but he gave them but a glance, and then fixed his eyes on the ground below.

Down he went, wings whining in the terrific rush of air, and the stick shaking under his steel grip. But, though acutely conscious of the excess strain of the battered plane, he grimly held it in its dive toward the Black Hawk's drome.

And then, when he was less than five thousand feet above the field, and a swarm of figures were gazing at him with up-turned faces, he twisted sharply around in the seat and looked back.

High above him, swinging down in lazy gliding circles was the bomber. Further south five more were nosing down out of the cloud layer.

Snapping his eyes to the front again, he tensed every muscle and fiber of his entire being.

"Okay, fellow," he grated. "Let's go now!"

As the last word spilled off his lips he hauled back on the

stick with every ounce of his strength, and stepped hard on right rudder.

For one split moment of hell the nose refused to come up. Then like a gale-bent limb whipping back into place, the nose shot up to level keel and went screaming around to the right. Before it had made three-quarters of the turn, Dusty checked it and sent it rocketing earthward again, straight for a range of rocky, scrub-growth covered hills.

Behind him the savage yammer of machine-gun fire blasted out. But he did not once turn his head to look.

He held the Silver Flash in its wire screaming plunge for the hill range.

Out the corner of his eye he saw armored cars rushing along the roads toward the hill range, and little tongues of jetting flame spat up at him from their dull glistening sides. But his speed was too great and the range to far, with the result that the Black gunners simply wasted hundreds of rounds of perfectly good ammunition.

Now the crest of the hill range, was less than a hundred feet below him. Hands rock steady, he eased the nose up and banked southwest along the range.

Foot by foot the Silver Flash lost flying speed. It was a matter of seconds now.

Spinning around in the seat he took one last look behind him. A mile away the armored cars were raising great clouds of dust on the dirt roads. Above them, twin engines roaring a mighty tune, the bomber was sweeping down.

Dusty grinned.

Then with a flash movement of the stick and rudder he whipped the plane up on right wing-tip, let it sideslip down the far side of the hill range. Its wheels grazed the tips of the scrub trees. And then, as a small clearing shot underneath him, he pulled the nose up to a sharp stall, braced himself and buried his head in his arms.

ONE, TWO—THREE seconds ticked by. Then, as though suspending wires had been cut, the Silver Flash mushed down wing first into the clearing.

Split seconds later Dusty's head was filled with the crash and ripping of twisting, crumpling metal. An unseen giant hurled him against the side of the cockpit, jerked him back and hurled him against the other side. Something smashed through the glass cowling and brushed painfully across the bullet crease on his shoulder.

Black oblivion speckled with a million stars of colored light swirled about him, and heaven and earth seemed to explode in one terrific crescendo of thunderous sound.

A few moments later a great heavy silence settled over everything.

Stunned, pains shooting through him from head to foot, he slowly lowered his arms. About him was nothing but an interlocking mass of branches, twigs and brownish green leaves.

Gasping with pain he slowly crawled through the smashed cowling and slid down a crumpled wing to the ground.

For a few seconds he was forced to lay there, fighting for breath and struggling to rid his spinning brain of the great black cloud engulfing it.

But presently, as distant sounds came to him, he staggered to his feet, lurched over to the shattered cockpit and thrust his right hand down in through the jagged hole in the cowling.

Numbed fingers groped along the side of the cockpit, fastened over the signal pistol and pulled it free from its clamps.

Examining it a second to make sure it was loaded, he reeled back a couple of paces, and pointed the thing at the split and leaking fuel tank just back of the engine.

"So long, old gal!" he grunted thickly.

He pulled the trigger. The big muzzle spat out a ball of green fire. The ball smacked into the leaking fuel tank. For a second it made a sharp hissing sound, then a sheet of flame leaped out and spread rapidly along the fuel-drenched fuselage.

Tossing the signal pistol into the flames, Dusty turned and went stumbling and sliding down the side of the hill, body crouched low and well under the overhanging branches of the scrub trees.

Not until he was across the valley and scrambling over the crest of an opposite hill did he slacken his pace. Sinking slowly to the ground, he wiggled under some bushes and looked back.

The small clearing on the opposite hillside was now a raging inferno that was spreading out like spilled oil, and consuming everything within reach of its licking red tongues.

So great was the intensity of the flames that the Silver Flash was completely hidden from view.

As he watched, a lump rose in his throat. He clenched his teeth, and dug his fingers into the soft ground.

"A hell of an end for it!" he groaned.

Suddenly, the roar of a plane overhead made him roll over on his back. Circling down as low as its pilot dared, was the Black bomber. And as Dusty squinted his eyes and peered hard he saw a black-uniformed figure shove back the cockpit cowling, lean out of it and fix powerful binoculars on the raging flames below. The Black Hawk.

Absently swabbing the blood from his face, he watched the giant plane swing slowly around the spot. Then a few moments later he heard a great clattering sound at the eastern end of the valley.

Even as he rolled over on his side and peered through the maze of underbrush, he knew exactly what he would see. And he was right. Churning up the valley in follow the leader formation were three of the Blacks' speedy armored cars.

But they were not so very speedy just now. In fact, the ground was so rough and brush-clogged that they were barely able to move through it.

Eventually, though, they reached a point below the blazing hillside, and came to a stop. Steel doors swung open and soldiers piled out. They scrambled up toward the dames.

But they were only able to get just so far before the terrific heat sent them scurrying down again. Going over to their cars they pulled out extinguisher tanks, strapped them to their backs and started climbing again.

But the thin stream of fire-extinguishing chemicals was useless against the raging fire. Relentlessly it crept down the hillside, forcing them steadily back, until at last they broke and ran for their cars.

A moment later engines roared, gears clashed, and all three of the cars careened around.

At the end of the valley, Dusty saw them stop. A soldier got out of the first one and climbed to the roof. Unfurling two small orange flags he started signalling to the bomber circling over head. After a few minutes he tucked the flags under his arm and climbed down into the car.

Engines making enough racket to match the thunder of the plane overhead, the cars rolled onward and lost themselves to Dusty's view.

Still hugging the ground, and not daring to move, he watched the bomber make one last circle of the flaming spot and then veer around to the south.

Heaving a weary sigh, he rolled over on his back, and closed his smarting eyes.

"And when you rats come back to make sure, he breathed softly, "Mrs. Ayres' little boy, Dusty, will be where you'd never figure him to be—and how!"

CHAPTER 8
BLACK TARMAC

NOT DARING to keep his eyes closed for long, lest he fall into an exhausted sleep, he soon opened them and rolled over on his stomach. His head ached horribly, and he suddenly remembered that he had not eaten for hours.

But with a grim shrug he dismissed all that from his thoughts. There was nothing he could do about it now. As a matter of fact, there wasn't anything he could do, except wait for the shadows of evening to creep across the countryside.

To move now, was to beg the Blacks to take him prisoner. And above all he had to avoid that final catastrophe.

For perhaps two hours he stayed right where he was. And then, when the shadows of evening closed over the landscape, he slowly got to this feet, flexed his stiff muscles, and went jog-trotting down the hill.

Continually checking his course with the aid of a small pocket compass, he held steady for an hour. When he caught the glimpse of flickering lights in the distance, he slowed down to a walk and veered his course toward the west.

He was on flat country now; the hill range was far behind him. A small village loomed up in the darkness off to his left. He skirted it stealthily and kept on going to the southwest.

Finally, when he had crept up to the crest of the slight rise in the ground, he sank down on hands and knees and studied the scene ahead through narrowed eyes.

Less than two hundred yards in front of him was the dim-ly-lighted drome of the Black Hawk. By straining his eyes he could just make out the shadowy blur of planes lined up on the tarmac. And at intervals he saw the silhouettes of guards against the dim background.

Longingly he stared at the planes. So near they were, yet so far. If he could only get one of them. Once he was in the air it wouldn't matter. Let them bums try to catch him.

He shook his head. He was straining his luck as it was. Before he could get within fifty feet of the nearest plane, a dozen Black guards would have their rifles trained on him. Nope, his only chance lay in the radio shack. Just two minutes in there and he'd be able to flash his warning back to G.H.Q.—warning of the most gigantic military maneuver ever attempted in the history of the world.

The very thought of it made him pause and consider the crazy diagram stamped on his brain. Had he figured it right? Was its significance really clear to him? After all, it was only guesswork on his part.

"I know I'm right!" he gritted savagely. "Hell, it can't be anything else."

Jerking his automatic from his breeches pocket, he curled a finger about the trigger and started to slowly circle the southern rim of the drome.

A thousand times his tensed nerves seemed ready to snap, and send him haywire. And a thousand times it was all he could do to stop himself from breaking into a mad dash for the small, stone-walled radio hut, on the east side of the field.

Twice he thought he saw the tall form of the Black Hawk go striding by one of the open and lighted hangar doorways. Instinctively he snapped up his gun and framed it on the figure. But sane reason prevented him from pulling the trigger.

The Hawk was no longer important to him now. Five hours ago he would have pounced upon the man and beaten the truth from his ugly lips with the butt of his automatic. But now that wasn't necessary. A few words of the Hawk in the earphones, and some furious thinking on Dusty's part had given him the answer he had been seeking ever since he pried the torn diagram out of the toe of the dead Strickland's shoe.

Virtually pressing his body into the ground, he edged toward the radio shack inch by inch and foot by foot. When it was less than fifty yards away, a motionless blur to his right suddenly whirled into action.

For one split second Dusty caught the dull glint of blue steel. The crack of a rifle belt snapping back was like the sound of Doomsday in his ears.

ACTION PRECEDED thought. Like a shot Dusty hurled his body sidewise, gun arm upraised. There was a grunt, and a gurgle. He saw big lips open to let out a following shout; saw a rifle muzzle swinging around toward him.

For at the same instant, even while still clear of the ground, he brought down his gun hand with every ounce of his strength.

Metal smashed into solid bone beneath the coarse skull cap. A faint sigh escaped through the parted lips of the Black sentry. Then the rifle slipped from his fingers, and his tall figure melted to the ground.

Grabbing the rifle with one hand, Dusty snaked his gun arm around the toppling Black, held him a second, then eased him down to the ground.

Placing the rifle beside him, he bent over the sentry, gun raised for another blow. But a close look at the ugly face made him lower his gun. No second tap on the head was needed. It would be many hours before the limp sentry would open his eyes again.

Dusty hugged the ground beside the Black for a few moments.

Then, as nothing else moved, he got to his feet and crept on toward the rear of the radio hut.

Five minutes later he was hugging the deep darkness of the rear wall. A faint shaft of light cut through a small window into the darkness. When he reached it, he slowly peered around the edge of the sill.

At first he saw only a room full of radio and wireless instruments. But a split second later he saw the back of a Black radio sergeant.

The man was perched on a stool in the far corner, phones clamped to his ears, and the upper part of his body hunched forward over the transmitter and receiving panels.

Dusty smiled grimly and took a tighter grip on the butt of his automatic. For several seconds he stood motionless and peered intently toward the group of buildings just back of the hangar line. Several indistinct figures were moving about, but not one of them came toward his side of the drome.

"Okay, fellow!" he grunted under his breath. "It's now or never!"

Crouching down, he scurried past the window, and around the corner to the door. Gun ready, he curled the fingers of his other hand about the knob and turned it gently.

Then, so slow that it seemed he wasn't even moving, he pushed the door open and snaked his body inside. Once the door was behind him he darted forward one quick step, and leaped the rest of the way.

Too late, the radio sergeant heard the scuffing of shoes on the floor behind him. As he twisted around on his stool, Dusty's gun barrel caught him square behind the right ear. Eyes wide open, and a silly expression spreading over his hatchet face, the Black keeled over backward like a wet sack of meal.

As he fell, Dusty snatched the earphones from his head, adjusted them on himself and bent over the transmission panel. Even as the sergeant's unconscious body hit the floor, Dusty was spinning the wave-length dial. With his other hand he tuned up maximum volume.

That other Black stations would pick him up, he knew full well. But, if only he could get through to Washington H.Q. first, it didn't matter what happened later.

A green signal light on the panel blinked rapidly. He snatched up the transmitter.

"Washington… Washington H.Q.," he called breathlessly. "This is Captain Ayres. Listen, the—"

A click in the phones cut him off. His heart plunged down to his boots. With trembling fingers he readjusted the dial reading. God be praised… the green light was blinking again.

"Washington H.Q.!" he called wildly. "Ayres speaking… send out a general alarm. The Blacks are planning to attack at—"

Crack!

A metallic wasp zipped past Dusty's head and smacked into the radio panel. Instantly there were three faint pops as three tubes exploded.

Crack!

The radio panel split straight through the middle and a thread of thick yellow smoke oozed upward. Dusty froze motionless, his hand halfway to his automatic.

"Stop!"

CHOKING BACK a groan, he slowly pivoted—to glare into the eyes of the Black Hawk. He stood in the open doorway, a gun clutched in his right fist.

For a second there was dead silence as the pair locked eyes. Then with a grating chuckle the Hawk snaked forward and snatched up Dusty's gun with his free hand. Dropping it in his pocket, he pulled a chair around with his foot and sat down. Not for one instant did his gun move away from the Yank's chest.

"And so we meet again, Captain Ayres," he purred softly.

Dusty didn't say anything. Face a mask, eyes glaring, he stood like a statue of stone. The Black Hawk patted his gun with his free hand and widened his smirk.

"It was clever, crashing and firing your plane, Captain," he said. "But it did not mislead me. I knew you are not the type to give up so easily, so, I simply waited for you."

Dusty licked his lips.

"Yeah?" he asked. "How'd you know I'd seek you out? Hell, you're not that important to me."

The other wagged his head tauntingly.

"Didn't you tell General Billings that you wanted to find me?"

Dusty's face darkened as he thought of the spy he'd shot.

"Oh, your spy told you in his last message, eh?" he snapped. "Well, he won't be telling you anything more."

"It doesn't matter," shrugged the Hawk. "We have other agents. The loss of one does not worry me. In a way, he deserved to die. He would have made things more difficult if he had killed you."

The Yank frowned in spite of himself.

"Yes," continued the Black Hawk, as though he hadn't paused. "With you dead it would have been hard to find out the exact truth."

Dusty laughed.

"I like riddles," he snapped. "But I'll have to give up on that one. What's the answer?"

"The answer is that you are going to give me a little information, Captain Ayres," replied the Black quietly. "At eleven o'clock this morning, or shortly thereafter, you aided an American spy in making his escape. He died in your arms. Of that I am positive, although I believed him dead as he went down by parachute. But—"

"So you were the rat that tried to shoot him after he bailed out!" blazed Dusty, swaying forward on the balls of his feet. "Why you dirty, low—!"

The gun was jabbed toward him.

"Move and you'll regret it. Yes, I was that other pilot. Unfortunately I could not remain to engage you. But that spy died in your arms. A report I received from an agent, who later examined the body—and incidentally put that artillery officer out of our way—convinces me that the spy talked before he died. What did he say, Captain—and what did you cut out of the toe of his right shoe?"

The last was spoken slowly, and with measured emphasis. Feigning a puzzled expression, the Yank shrugged.

"I'm still punk at guessing the answers to riddles," he snapped.

Rage smoldered in the Hawk's eyes, and his forefinger tightened about the trigger of the gun.

"Perhaps you forget, Captain," he purred harshly, "that it would be very simple for me to put a bullet in your heart."

Dusty grinned inwardly. He knew damned well that if the Hawk wasn't worried about something, he would have shot him minutes ago.

"I'm not forgetting," he said evenly. "But I still can't answer your riddle."

The Hawk gave him a long, shrewd glance. Dusty fought to keep the puzzled expression on his face, and prayed fervently that the truth was not showing in his eyes. Presently the Black spoke again.

"I'm giving you your choice of life or death. And I promise you that death will not be by a bullet. It will be the most terrible death you could possibly imagine. Now, tell me—did that American spy talk, and what did you take from his right shoe?"

Dusty looked him straight in the eye.

"I'm scared stiff about dying," he said. "So I guess I'd better tell you."

The other's eyes widened and he leaned forward eagerly.

"Yes, yes?" he got out harshly. "Tell me!"

The Yank hesitated, and curled his lips back in a slow grin.

"Well, he said to me that if I wanted a drink I'd find a quart in his right shoe. So I cut open the shoe and finished the bottle. Not bad stuff, either!"

A roaring curse spilled off the Hawk's lips. He leaped forward and swung the gun. Dusty blocked part of the blow, but it nevertheless sent him reeling back against the opposite wall.

For an instant he poised to hurl himself at the snarling Black. But the unwavering gun muzzle fixed dead upon him cooled his passion. Instead, he grinned defiantly.

"That's your style!" he grated. "You haven't the guts to try anything man to man. Go ahead and shoot, and I'll see you in hell!"

For one horrible second, Dusty's heart went cold from the sudden realization that his taunting rage was sealing his doom. Insane with anger, the Black Hawk was going to shoot, regardless.

Body instinctively braced for the expected bullet, Dusty watched through glaring eyes as the Black battled with his own emotions. And then suddenly the Hawk's tensed figure relaxed and the gleam of savage hatred died from his eyes.

In spite of himself, Dusty could not check the tiny sigh of relief that rippled off his lips. For a moment his knees went water weak, and the room swam. But almost instantly, he got a grip on himself.

"Well?" he asked easily, "are you going to shoot?"

The other shook his head.

"No, it will not be by a bullet."

Keeping his gun trained on Dusty, the Black edged over to the wall and jabbed his thumb against a bell button. He held it pressed until there were the sounds of running feet outside, in the darkness. Presently the two apelike Black mechanics entered and saluted the Hawk with the peculiar Invader salute—

right forearm raised up and the outward facing palm of the hand on a line with the shoulder.

The Hawk returned the salute and then barked an order that Dusty did not understand. But he did a moment later as the mechanics pinned him against the wall and searched him systematically.

Holding his breath for fear that they might find the green bead jammed in the seam in his breeches pocket, he offered no resistance whatsoever. And finally when they backed away from him scowling, and shook their heads at the Black Hawk, his heart leaped with joy. They had not found the bead.

After a moment or two of silence, the Hawk snarled some more orders. Again the mechanics grabbed Dusty. But this time they did not pin him against the wall.

Steel fingers curled about his upper arms, they virtually yanked him off his feet and propelled him through the door, into the darkness outside.

Looking to neither the left nor the right, they hurried him across the drome to a bomb dugout on the opposite side. Jerking him to a stop.

One of them released his hold and lifted open the heavy steel-reinforced bulkhead door.

"I leave you to your thoughts for a while," came the Hawk's chuckling voice from in back of Dusty. "And also, to a little surprise!"

As the last word died to the echo, a battering ram crashed into the small of Dusty's back. With a cry of alarm, he flung out his hands for a grip on something. But they were instantly paralyzed by crushing blows from the two Black mechanics, and he went spinning and bumping down the dugout stairs. And as he crashed against a rough wood floor, the bulkhead door banged shut, and a heavy bolt clanked into place.

CHAPTER 9
THE GREEN BEAD

S TUNNED, DUSTY lay gasping for breath in that pit of enveloping darkness. A dozen times unconsciousness reached out to spread its shroud over his pain-wracked body. But each time the fighting instinct within him beat it back.

And then, finally, he crawled up onto his hands and knees, lurched over against the steps and stared about him.

It was then that he realized that the dugout was not as black as it had at first seemed. As a matter of fact, it was flooded with a faint light that seeped down through a cross-shaped window high up in the domed ceiling.

For a moment, he wondered dully about that fact. How the hell should there be light, when it was night outside? And then, as the faint light seemed to flicker, he knew and understood. The dugout was close to the hangar line, and the light coming through the dome window was the faint reflection of the lights in the hangars.

That settled in his throbbing brain, he began a slow tour of the walls. Halfway around, he bumped into the only piece of furniture in the place—a low plank bench.

Too exhausted to continue around the bare interior, he sank

down on the bench, leaned his head back against the wall, and stared moodily up toward the cross window.

For the want of something better to do, he toyed with the possibility of trying to make his escape through the window. But really serious consideration of the idea forced him to abandon it completely.

In the first place it was a good twelve feet beyond his reach. And in the second place it was made up of thick glass and many crisscross steel bars. Hell, naturally it would be like that. What good would a bomb dugout be if a bomb could come down through a flimsy window?

With an unhappy sigh, he allowed his eyes to close. Better to relax and rest while he may. He probably wouldn't be there long. He guessed that much from the Hawk's parting remark. But the Hawk had also said something about a surprise. Surprise?

He opened his eyes and stared absently at the opposite wall. He couldn't guess the answer. Hell, what a sweet jam he was in now! One more minute and he would have been able to send the truth back to Washington H.Q.—the true meaning of that torn diagram.

At that moment, he sat up straight. The bolt had been jerked free in the bulkhead door. The door was being opened!

A sharp cry rang out. Almost immediately it was followed by a scuffle of feet and a clawing of hands as a figure came hurtling down the steps.

Not making a move, Dusty watched it literally bounce on the floor, and roll over. The figure was clad in the uniform of a Black soldier.

Straining his eyes, he stared at the man who was now groaning and rubbing his big hands about his head. Presently the Black sat up slowly. He turned his head toward Dusty. Dark eyes blinked and squinted, then widened in dumbfounded amazement.

Dusty gasped. The Black soldier was not a Black soldier at all. He was an American—a man with whom Dusty had gone through the fires of hell on two different occasions—Agent 10 of the U.S. Intelligence Department!

At first Dusty refused to believe his own eyes. But as the other grinned, he knew beyond all possible doubt that he was looking at the man known as Agent 10, and whom he secretly knew to be the only son of General Horner, Chief of U.S. Intelligence.

He shot off the bench and knelt down beside the man.

"You!" he gasped. "Hell, I thought you were still in Washington! What?"

"A long story, Ayres," the other grunted. "I should be in the States, but I figured that I could fool the Blacks and come back here again. Well, I was wrong. Guess they've had their eye on me ever since you flew me out of that last jam. I got hold of something big, and they nabbed me two hours later."

Dusty put his hand over the other's mouth.

"Not so loud," he snapped. "We don't know if this place has ears."

The other shook off Dusty's hand.

"It hasn't," he said. "I spent most of the day here. It's just a parking place for their prisoners, until they take them over to

96

their torture chamber. They don't go in for simple dictaphone stuff, if that's what you mean. They've got other ways to—But, say! What are you doing here?"

DUSTY GRIMACED. "Oh, I was just checking up on a hunch, and I stuck my head into a noose. But you said something about getting hold of something big. What was it?"

The Yank agent hesitated, and scowled down at the floor.

"Damn right it was big!" he muttered. "And our boys are going to beat the Black army tomorrow and the day after."

Dusty nodded.

"Maybe," he said softly. "If they find out in time."

The other jerked his head around and stared at him.

"What the hell do you mean?"

The pilot hesitated a second, then bent his head close.

"The green bead and the torn map didn't get through!" he said.

The effect of the words made the Intelligence man stiffen as though he had been suddenly pierced by a bullet.

"How—good God!"

"Strickland died in my arms," Dusty went on.

Then he told Agent 10 of his experiences in a few short sentences.

"I didn't catch on to the real meaning of the thing until a few hours ago," he finished up. "It was the figures that stumped me. But as soon as the thought came to me that they were dates, the rest was simple!"

"Simple?" cut in the other with a groan. "God, it's hellish. Tomorrow they spring the trap!"

"Maybe!" grunted Dusty. "But let me check with you to make sure I got it all. The map is like this—" He drew a hasty sketch of the design which he had burned into his memory that morning.

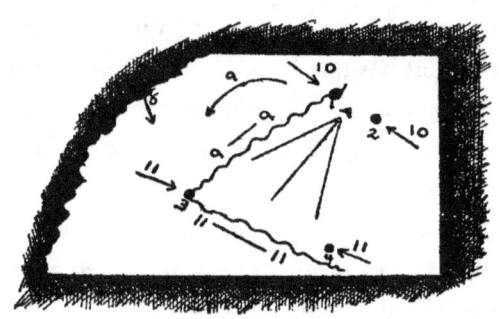

"The wavy line, 99, is the gas curtain they sent up today. Right? Figure 1 is the northern point where Maine joins New Hampshire. In other words Z-10 area. Figure 2 is the Bath, Maine, area. Three is the Buffalo area, and 4 is New York. On the tenth, tomorrow, the Blacks will move against Z-10 by land, and Bath area by sea.

"By doing that they plan to pull our reserves up north. And when they do that their surprise army will smash through Buffalo and head for New York. And New York will be attacked from the sea also. That'll be on the eleventh—day after tomorrow. The number 8 on that diagram represented the date reserves would be started toward the Buffalo area. And the curved 9 line represented the main reserve army that I saw today, moving behind the gas curtain screen toward the Buffalo area.

"In other words the Z-10 and Bath attacks are only gigantic fakes to pull our armies and sea power up north. Then they'll cut across from Buffalo to New York, and try to bottle up the whole works. There—am I right?"

Dusty asked the last question eagerly. The secret agent, who had been listening in a dazed sort of way, slowly nodded his head.

"You are—and neat work," he grunted. "I drew that diagram myself, but—"

The man paused and a shaky hopeless laugh rattled in his throat.

"What the hell's the good of checking with me?" he groaned. "It won't help, knowing that you figured it out right."

The pilot smiled grimly, and slowly bunched both hands into steel-knotted fists.

"I'll at least know I'm telling the truth, when I finally get word through to G.H.Q.," he breathed softly.

"Get word through?" echoed the other in a defeated tone that sent a little pang of pity through Dusty's heart. "Even if a miracle happens, and you do—it'll be too late."

For a moment Dusty made no comment. The other's resigned attitude surprised him more than a little. In the past, Agent 10 had never been like this. He had been the spark plug of their adventures—a man totally devoid of nerves.

Dusty gripped the man's shoulder.

"Chin up, fellow!" he said earnestly. "We're far from licked yet!"

The other heaved a sigh.

"I'm not thinking of us!" he grunted. "I know we're sunk. I'm thinking of the others. God, I was only able to stand what they did to me this morning, because I thought that Strickland had gotten through."

"ABOUT THIS Strickland," cut in Dusty quickly. "As I told you, his cousin said that he wasn't a pilot. And what about that green bead? That's the one thing I can't figure."

Agent 10 pursed his lips.

"I didn't know much about Strickland," he said. "None of us know much about each other in this service. Only learned his name last night. The green bead is the way one agent identifies himself to another in case of emergency. We are never captured with it on our person.

"That's the one order we can never disobey—to destroy it if we're captured. In that way the Blacks have never been able to catch on to the idea. They've never seen one of the things. And, as far as I know, they don't even know of the idea. They—"

The man suddenly stopped and grabbed Dusty's arm.

"My God!" he cried excitedly. "You said you destroyed that diagram map, but—what about the bead? Did they get it?"

Dusty had to shake off the trembling fingers in order to dig the bead out of the breeches pocket seam.

"Nope," he said, and dropped it in the other's hand.

Agent 10 uttered a low moan of relief as he fondled the bead. Dusty frowned.

"I don't think so much of the idea," he said. "I'd say you're taking chances on whether or not the other chap with a bead really is one of your gang. A common, ordinary green bead isn't so hard to—"

"But it isn't a common, ordinary bead," the secret agent cut in. "Look!"

Placing the bead between his two thumbs he twisted sharply. Then he separated his thumbs and two halves of the bead dropped into the palm of his left hand. With his right forefinger he poked them over so that the flat sides showed. Stamped in each flat surface was a tiny white figure 8.

"Strickland's number," murmured Agent 10 as Dusty squinted at the numerals. "As an extra precaution there is a secret question that each of us can ask about the other's number. The answer we get will tell us the truth. But no one will ever ask the question of this number again."

As he spoke, Agent 10 quickly placed the two halves on the floor and ground them to green dust beneath his heel. A puff from his lips and the green dust disappeared.

"I did that to mine this morning," he grunted.

"So Strickland really was an agent?" muttered Dusty, as though still unable to believe it. "Funny, though, his cousin getting that letter—and about his flying, too!"

"Nothing funny at all," the other replied. "You don't advertise enlistment in the Intelligence Department, even to your cousin. But Strickland was a pilot, right enough. His cousin just didn't know what he was talking about, that's all."

For a moment or two they both sat there in brooding silence.

"Tell me more about that diagram," said Dusty after awhile. "I want the whole story so I can convince G.H.Q."

Again Agent 10's face took on the expression of utter defeat and hopelessness.

"No sense in hoping this time, Ayres," he said dully. "The Blacks will probably change their plans, knowing that you got hold of the map."

"But that's the idea!" interrupted Dusty. "They don't know. That's what has them worried. I'll bet my shirt on it. Hell, I'd be dead now if they knew the truth. So tell me the rest, and we can figure from there."

Dusty's words seemed to cheer Agent 10 a little.

"Not much to tell," he said. "By a chance meeting I contacted Strickland soon after I got through. He'd been on this side for a week as one of their civilian air mechanics. Said that something was in the wind. Didn't know just what, but said the answer was in the area H.Q.

"As a civilian mechanic he couldn't get near the place. As an ordinary soldier, I could, and did. One look at a marked-up wall map was all I needed. The whole plan was pin-pointed out."

THE MAN smiled bitterly. "It was bait!" he grated after a while. "Live bait—and I took it hook, line and sinker. The rats had put their secret right in plain view, hoping I'd walk into their trap. I did, but I damn near beat them at their own game.

"I made that diagram. Just as I finished they closed in on me. I tore off a blank piece of the paper and scaled it through a window. Like I was tossing it to an accomplice. That made them hesitate long enough for me to dive through an opposite window and run for it.

"A bit of luck put Strickland in my path. He faked a charge

at me, and I dropped the wadded diagram, and dodged around him. In the excitement to get me, which they did about two minutes later, Strickland scooped up the wad and started his get-away by air. God, if only he could have crashed through!"

Jack-knifing his knees, the man rested his elbows on them and cupped his hands about his chin. Eyes narrowed, he stared dully ahead. Dusty studied him keenly, a faint perplexed frown knitting his brows together.

"A funny question," he suddenly blurted out. "But just why are you still alive? I thought that—"

"A spy was shot on sight?" the other finished with out turning his head. "They usually are, unless it's believed that he'll spill information. And that's what the rats figured about me, curse their rotten hides. I wish to hell they had shot me!"

"Nonsense," Dusty snapped angrily. "You're not that type. Licking these bums is a pushover job for us. We've done it before, haven't we? Well, we'll do it again!"

The other turned his head just enough to stare into Dusty's face.

"Thanks, Ayres, thanks a lot," he said thickly. "I pray to God you can get through somehow. But you'll see what I mean, very soon. Hell, let's talk about something else!"

A strange undertone in the man's voice made fingers of ice clutch at Dusty's heart. He shook them off with a muttered curse and started to speak again, but checked himself quickly. The bulkhead bolt had clanked back, and the door was being lifted open.

A brilliant beam of light shot down the dugout steps. Three

pairs of heavy boots thumped behind it. And presently, preceded by two armed guards, the Black Hawk came down the steps.

Holding the light so that its beam ricocheted off the dome ceiling, and lighted up the whole place, the Black pilot grinned mockingly and bowed stiffly from the waist.

"And now this pleasant little reunion must come to an end," he purred. Then looking straight at Dusty. "Did I not promise you a surprise, Captain?"

The Yank pilot matched the other's look and grinned also.

"Thanks," he said. "And you've got a little surprise coming to you, too!"

For a second the Black's eyes narrowed questioningly. Then he shrugged, and laughed aloud.

"An extreme pleasure," he said easily. Then bending his cruel, ugly face close to Agent 10, "A double pleasure, eh, swine? Even more than I enjoyed this morning!"

"Damn you!" howled the other, and flung himself forward.

Dusty yelled a warning, but it was too late. One of the Black guards swung his rifle and the barrel smashed against Agent 10's head with a sickening sound. Hands outstretched for the Hawk's neck, the Yank secret agent seemed to suddenly relax in midair. Then he crumpled to a heap on the floor.

Dusty started to leap himself, but the other guard jabbed him savagely in the pit of the stomach, and he went reeling back, choking for breath.

The Hawk barked an order at the guards. One of them picked up Agent 10 as though he were a babe, and slung him across his massive shoulders. The other prodded Dusty in the back.

And with the Black Hawk bringing up the rear, they all trudged up the dugout steps.

CHAPTER 10
SATAN'S ARMCHAIR

UPON REACHING the drome level the guards turned sharp right and proceeded along the edge of the field toward a group of buildings at the eastern end of the hangar line. Biting his lip against the pain of the gun muzzle jammed cruelly in the small of his back, Dusty cast his eyes about.

Lined up in front of the hangars were an array of enemy ships, from the fleet Darts of the Hawk's unit, to giant flying-wing germ and gas bombers. In fact, there were so many different types that they extended past the hangar line itself and occupied most of the western border of the drome.

Mechanics in black jumpers were swarming all over them. Others were dollying germ and gas tanks out to the bigger ships. And still more were gingerly easing deadly aerial torpedoes into underslung wing cradles. A great sky armada of death was being groomed for its hell-raid!

Where would it strike—at Z-10, or the Buffalo area? Or would it strike from the sea at Bath, or New York?

The questions burned through Dusty's brain as he stared at the nest of death-dealing, black-winged vultures. And his heart ached as he thought of the thousands upon thousands of unsuspecting Yanks who were to be the victims.

"The Blacks would not be fools enough to attack the Z-10 area."

Dusty groaned as General Billings' words came back to him. That was exactly the idea of the plan.

Realizing that an attack against the Z-10 area was military suicide, the Blacks were going to fake one, draw the American armies up into New England for a crushing counter-attack, and then bottle them up by smashing through the Buffalo area and across New York State and Pennsylvania to New York City.

A bold, almost insane plan for any attacking force. Yet, fantastic and crazy as it seemed to Dusty's military mind, he realized that its chances of success were well within the realm of possibility.

Once the fake Z-10 sucked the American forces up into New England, and the Atlantic battle fleet was drawn up to the defense of the Bath area, it would be a military race by sea, land and air to the greatest prize of all—the City of New York. New York—the throbbing center of the financial, industrial and business arteries of the entire United States.

Dusty raised his eyes toward the southern heavens. An eerie chill went through him.

The gas curtain still billowed upward. He could see it beyond the dull red glare of heavy H.E. guns in action far to the south.

Almost simultaneously he became conscious of the fact that the rumbling in his ears he had believed to be an aftermath of the terrific blow in the stomach, was the rolling sound of heavy cannonading. The fake attack against Z-10 was already underway!

"Yes, the attack has started."

Dusty turned his head to find the Hawk at his side. The intensity of his stare made Dusty's heart jump. How long had the Hawk been there? Had he read anything in the expression on the Yank's face?

With an effort he steeled himself.

"Just wasting ammunition," he countered. "You couldn't even dent our lines there."

"Ah!"

The sharp exclamation caused the blood in Dusty's veins to run cold.

"Ah!" repeated the Hawk, his smiling lips curling back over fang teeth. "So the spy did tell you something?"

"Still talking riddles, eh?" Dusty snapped back at him.

"No," purred the other softly. "Our agent that you killed told me of your conversation with General Billings. Didn't you realize that?"

"Yeah? Then why this old-home-week gathering, if you know everything?"

"When I captured you, I did not know," said the Hawk. "As a result of an error, by a man who has paid for it with his life, I did not get all of my agent's message until just a few minutes ago. So now, you will not have to tell me as much as I had planned."

"That'll be nice, won't it?" snorted Dusty.

"And simple, too," muttered the Hawk as he dropped back a few paces.

HIS GUARD grabbed Dusty by the shoulder and jerked

him to a halt. They were in front of a low-roofed, single-story building that, so far as Dusty could see, contained only one door and no windows. It was a log cabin structure, the logs being fastened together with iron ribs. Yet, strangely enough, the door instead of being made of wood was made of solid copper with riveted hinges.

Stepping around the guards and their charges, the Hawk pulled a bunch of keys from his pocket, selected one and fitted it into the narrow keyhole that Dusty had not noticed until that minute. After a sharp twist of the key, the Black shoved open the door, and motioned the guards inside.

With the gun muzzle digging into his back deeper than ever, Dusty stepped into a dark room. He heard the door close behind him, heard the click of a switch, and instantly there was brilliant light.

It was so brilliant that it blinded Dusty, and for several moments he was unable to see a single thing. Eventually, his eyes refocused and he looked about him.

His first impression was that he was standing in the main room of a power generating plant. The wall seemed covered with every conceivable instrument known to electrical science. Then suddenly, as his eyes picked out several relay boxes, transformers and speaker units, he realized that the place was the main signal station.

But he was wrong.

The Hawk had been watching his face, and had evidently read his thoughts—told him so in his next words.

"No, Captain, you couldn't guess. This happens to be one of

our portable experimental plants. A place where we experiment on various ideas that require either mechanical or electrical power. For instance, see that object in the far corner?"

The man paused long enough to point at what looked to Dusty like a bed spring bent into the shape of a chair.

"My own idea," continued the Black Hawk with unconcealed pride in his tone. "A few perfections required, to be true. Nevertheless, quite practical for immediate purpose. Though I haven't given it a name, the success of my experiments induce me to name it the Talking Chair. Here, I will demonstrate the connection."

He barked something at the guard who still held the unconscious Agent 10 slung across his shoulders. With a nod, the guard carried his burden over to the queer looking thing and dumped him into it in a sitting position. Then with brutal force, the guard ripped off the man's tunic and shirt, exposing him bare to the waistline.

It was then that Dusty saw the parallel rows of raw and bleeding welts across the man's chest. For a moment he saw red, and started to lurch forward, but the guard stopped him and held him in a grip of steel. Helpless, he stood there quivering with rage, and the other guard calmly went on with his work.

First he lashed Agent 10's wrists to the arms of the chair with steel mesh straps. In the same manner he secured the ankles to the lower part of the framework. And the third and last movement was to circle the man's neck with a strip of steel mesh and draw the head tight against the back of the frame.

That done, he saluted the Hawk and took up a position at Dusty's side.

Without so much as even looking at Dusty, the Hawk went over to a nearby table and picked up an oblong frame, the two ends of which were connected by several fine-drawn steel wires. Hooking one end over clamps of the right side of the queer chair back, he pressed the frame across Agent 10's bleeding chest and fastened it down with the clamp hooks on the left side of the chair back. The result was that now Agent 10's bare torso was completely encased in wire!

INSPECTING HIS work a second, the Hawk nodded his satisfaction, and walked over to a dial and rheostat panel on the side wall. His hand resting on a lever switch, he paused and grinned at Dusty.

"Your friend is asleep," he leered. "I will wake him up—so."

With a quick motion the Black slapped down the switch handle. Instantly a low-keyed humming sound reverberated through the room. Higher and higher it rose in pitch until it seemed to become a part of its own echo.

"Watch, Captain!" shouted the Hawk. "Watch your friend. See—he is waking up!"

With an effort Dusty tore his eyes from the Hawk's face and looked toward the wire chair. As he did, his blood froze in horror.

The wire frame pressed across Agent 10's chest was glowing red, the wires sinking into the yielding flesh like a hot iron sinking into snow. A moment later faint threads of smoke curled upward, and the man's body twitched and trembled convulsively. Then his whitened lips parted and a cry of mortal pain gushed from his throat.

As the cry died to an echo, there came to Dusty's ears the click of a switch and the wires ceased to glow red. But where they had burned into the raw flesh they still smoked faintly, and the nauseating stench in Dusty's nostrils made everything become a swirling, blurred mass before his eyes.

So this was what Agent 10 had meant when he'd said, "I know we're sunk, and you'll see what I mean very soon!" This was the torture chamber the man had been taken to that morning!

God, no wonder his usual indomitable spirit had been broken and crushed. With hope in his heart that his comrade operator, Strickland, had gotten through to the American side, Agent 10 had faced this horrible torture. And then, his body undoubtedly screaming with pain, he had learned the bitter truth from Dusty. Learned that all his sacrifices and all his suffering had gone for naught.

Through a swimming red haze, Dusty heard his own roaring voice.

"You rotten killer! Leave him alone. He can tell you nothing! He knows nothing!"

The smirk of a gloating maniac was on the Hawk's ugly face.

"It touches you, eh, Captain?" he sneered. "The dog is very stubborn. He refused to reveal the identity of other secret agents we believe to be in our midst. And so, regrettable as it seems, I must continue persuading him to talk."

Turning his back to Dusty, the Hawk walked over to the wire chair.

"And now, Agent 10," he sneered at the chalk faced, blazing-eyed man, "perhaps your tongue has loosened since this morning? Perhaps you will tell me of the other spies who roam among us?"

The helpless agent strained against his mesh bonds, and the voice that seemed to come from way down deep inside of him, shook with defiance.

"Do your damnedest—and go straight to hell!"

The Hawk stiffened, half raised a fist as though he were going to smash it into the man's face, then suddenly relaxed and lowered his hand.

"Still stubborn, eh?" he purred softly. "Well, I have said I would demonstrate my talking chair to Captain Ayres. And I consider it a promise."

Agent 10 roared a blistering curse at him and went limp from pain and exhaustion. The Hawk stood chuckling a moment then turned toward the control panel.

Held fast in the steel grip of his guards, Dusty nevertheless fought like an enraged tiger to break free. But it was but a waste of his own fast-waning strength.

The gash on his head burned like a live coal, and his breath came in jerky, whistling gasps. Through glazed eyes he saw the Hawk raise his claw hand for the switch lever. It was more than he could stand.

"Wait—wait," he choked out. "The man can tell you nothing. None of them know each other!"

"To hell with him, Ayres!" Agent 10's trembling voice called across the room. "Don't worry about me."

DUSTY DIDN'T even look toward him. His eyes were riveted on the Hawk's hand. If that switch handle went down again—

The Black let go of the switch handle and came over to him. So great was Dusty's sense of momentary relief, that he missed the gleam of evil cunning in the Hawk's deep-sunken jet-black eyes.

"So, your friend can tell me nothing, oh?" the man mused aloud, eyes boring into Dusty's face. "Perhaps you are right, Captain. As a matter of fact I am not particularly interested in what he might tell me. It is what you have to tell me!"

The last was spat out like machine-gun fire. Claw fingers were hooked in the loose front of Dusty's shirt, and he was half jerked off his feet as the Hawk bent his hatchet face close.

"Yes, what you have to tell me!" the man snarled. "Speak, and perhaps your friend will live!"

Dusty steeled himself, and looked at the man unblinking.

"Tell you what?" he grated. "I thought you said you knew everything!"

He held his breath while the other man paused.

"The truth," went on the man suddenly. "You learned about our secret attack—of how we plan to cut off America's armies. But, of one thing I must be sure—there was a period of thirty minutes this afternoon when we were unable to blanket out your wave-length. It was while you were climbing up through our smoke screen, which you thought would mislead us. Did you use your radio during that time? Did you warn your American G.H.Q.?"

"Keep your mouth shut, Ayres!"

Dusty heard Agent 10's voice. He was too occupied with his own reactions to the Hawk's words. He had guessed correctly! His life had been spared because the Blacks wondered if he had given a warning to his comrades. Thirty minutes when they had been unable to blanket out his wave-length.

Hell, during that time he hadn't even used the radio for fear of betraying his presence in the air. What a twist of fate. Thirty minutes of unsuspecting silence upon which now hung the life of Agent 10 and his own.

He grinned up into the leering, narrow-eyed face.

"Wouldn't you like to know?" he snorted.

The Hawk surprised him with a vigorous nod.

"Yes," he snarled. "Your life is in my hands, Captain. You mean nothing to me. But too much is at stake, now. Tell me the truth, or you shall watch your friend die before your eyes."

Keeping the mocking grin on his face, Dusty battled madly with his problem.

Should he lie and say that the Yanks had been informed? Should he tell the truth and admit that word had not been sent through? Or should he seal his lips and let the Hawk go on wondering? Which course to follow?

If he lied, what then? The fake attack was already underway. The Blacks would probably go through with their plan, and double the force of the blow at Buffalo—or at some other point.

And the Yanks, still ignorant of the double attack, would meet the same fate.

Or if he told the truth? It might save Agent 10's life, and his own. But he doubted that. The Hawk would never let them leave this room alive, once he was sure of the truth.

Besides their lives didn't matter, now. It was a case of thousands upon thousands of lives, not just two. The Blacks would be sure to strike, knowing that their terrible secret was safe.

Or should he keep them guessing—tell them nothing? THAT LAST thought made his heart beat rapidly. Perhaps it might delay them long enough so that some kind of miracle could happen, and the Yank forces be warned of the impending doom hovering about them.

Delay, at least, meant postponement of a crushing death. And the elements of time in the waging of war had often proved itself to be the difference between victory and defeat.

On impulse he made up his mind.

"That's another answer you'll have to guess!" he flung back into the Black's teeth.

Stark murder flared in the Hawk's eyes. With savage words that Dusty did not understand, he hurled him back against the guards and went over to the control panel.

"All right!" he screamed. "Watch him die!"

Down clicked the switch handle. Agent 10's body twitched and quivered. Yellow smoke rose up from the bleeding flesh of his chest. A sickening, sizzling sound filled the room. And above it came the harsh, rasping order of the Hawk.

"The truth! For the last time, the truth!"

For an instant Dusty's whirling brain seemed to go blank. From way off he heard the groaning cries of Agent 10. And as though he was looking into the pit of hell, itself, he saw the blood-drenched, smoking figure in the wire chair, quivering and jerking about in mortal agony. Then something seemed to snap inside of him and he forgot all else except that a brave man was slowly burning to death before his eyes.

"Stop—for God's sake stop! I'll—"

Shrill rage-filled words from Agent 10 stopped him.

"Ayres, don't tell them. For my sake, don't tell them!"

The tortured man's plea ringing in Dusty's throbbing ears seemed to suddenly engulf him in an ocean of seething flame. In that moment he ceased to be a human being. He became a raging, bellowing animal possessed of unlimited strength.

His blazing brain hardly registering the fact that his body was in motion, he lurched and twisted and kicked out with his right foot.

A voice screamed with pain, and steel fingers slipped from his right arm. Around he pivoted, his clenched fist coming like a flash of light. Knuckles crashed against jaw bone, and a white hot spear ripped up his forearm. Through blood-reddened eyes he saw a gun go spinning from the hands of one of the guards.

He lunged for it, caught it in mid-flight, jammed it against the black form which smashed into him and jerked the trigger.

The roar deafened him, and the downward crashing Black threw him off balance. Stumbling clear, he swung toward the moving blur of Hawk, racing for the door.

"No you don't!" he howled.

But as he tried to make his numbed fingers raise the gun up, and pull the trigger, the four walls seemed to cave in on him with a thunderous roar.

Through the red film he saw the other guard start swinging his gun for a second blow. Paralyzed muscles refused to obey—and then the whole world blew up inside his head.

CHAPTER 11
TALK OR DIE!

DULL, INCESSANT rumbling coming from a great way off finally caused Dusty to open his eyes. Brain still stunned, he stared up into a shadowy void. In a detached way he realized that he was still alive. The pain that seemed to pierce his body in a thousand different places proved that.

With a moan he closed his eyes and struggled to make his brain function properly. It was all he could do to stop himself into unconsciousness. But he fought against it.

When he again opened his eyes his brain had cleared. He was lying flat on his back and staring up at a dark, gray-painted ceiling. He started to sit up, groaned from the pain, and flopped back. On the third try he succeeded in propping himself up to a sitting position and wiggling his body back and forth so that he could brace it against the wall. But the effort set his head ringing with four alarm intensity, and everything became a swirling blur in front of him.

"Ayres! Thank God—thought you were dead!"

The whispered words on his right made him turn that way and strive desperately to pierce the swimming blur.

Presently he was able to see the blood-drenched figure of Agent 10 crumpled in the far corner of the room.

The man was lying on his right side, one arm pillowed under his head, and the other dangling down in a pool of blood on the floor. Glazed eyes met Dusty's, and bloodless lips twitched in a grimace.

The pilot summoned his strength, and crawled over on his hands and knees. But as he got close his heart seemed to stop beating. It seemed as if death was slowly reaching out its hand for Agent 10. The man's chest was a mass of raw, bleeding flesh. And in the depths of his eyes was the glassy look of a man living beyond his time.

Dusty tore off a piece of his own shirt and started to wipe the wounds. But Agent 10 winced and shook his head.

"Don't!" he got out faintly. "No use. I can't stand the pain. Listen—"

He choked and blood flecked the corners of his mouth. Dusty clenched his fists helplessly. There was absolutely nothing he could do.

"Listen, Ayres," the other gasped. "Don't tell—him. He's coming back. "Don't tell—the—swine!"

"I won't, fellow," Dusty promised by way of soothing him. "Now, take it easy—we're both going to need our strength."

The other stared at him vacantly, then slowly raised one hand.

"Hear that?" he murmured. "It's been going on for hours. I wonder—I wonder whether—?"

Dusty didn't notice that he had stopped talking, for his ears had suddenly become pitched to a heavy rumble in the distance. He turned his head, saw light streaming through a window and gasped aloud. He looked questioningly at Agent 10. The other's eyes, which had never left him, gleamed the answer. Then the bloodless lips moved to confirm it.

"The first attack. Over twelve hours ahead of time. It—must be noon, now. Noon of the tenth. I heard their planes leave— when it was still dark. Too bad—we did our best—tough luck!"

The eyes flickered closed.

"Hold it there, fellow!" Dusty called out in alarm. "There must be a way. I'll get you out."

DUSTY SCREWED around on his knees and looked wildly about the room. It contained only one window and one door. The window was high up, and well barred. The door was of iron reinforced oak. Even as he crawled over to it and grabbed the handle, he knew what to expect. The door was securely bolted on the other side.

Stumbling back, he slumped down beside the dying man, and stirred him gently.

"The Hawk, how long has he been gone?"

It seemed an eternity before the eyelids fluttered open.

"The Hawk?" faintly. "He didn't go with the others. He's still here. Heard him say—he was going to take you—with him— later. Heard him tell the guard outside!"

"But, where are we?" asked Dusty in desperation as the man's eyes started to close again.

"In prison block—behind the hangars. Tough—Ayres—

tough! But—its been aces knowing you. So long. They'll never—lick—America. Never!"

To get the last word out the man arched his bleeding chest and used up the last ounce of strength in his torn body. Then, as Dusty reached out comforting arms, he collapsed and lay still. With a choking sob, Dusty grabbed him.

"Agent 10—Horner—come back fellow!"

But the eyes did not open this time.

Strickland, Major Walker, Sergeant Crabtree, General Billings, Major Shelton and now Agent 10. All dead because of a green bead and a torn diagram map. There was only one left now—himself.

A wild laugh fell off his lips. Hell, he might as well be dead too. He had failed, failed miserably. The attack was over twelve hours underway. Right now the Yanks were being sucked up into the gigantic trap. Perhaps even the crash through the Buffalo area had been started. And he was a helpless prisoner.

Putting his hands against the floor for a brace, he slowly pushed himself up onto his feet. Teeth clenched, he turned toward the still American, and saluted stiffly.

"It should have been me, instead of you, Yank," he said. "But I pledge you my word, fellow, I'll kill him myself."

And then an ocean of misery swept over him, he stumbled over beside his silent friend and slumped down on the floor.

Suddenly the smack of the door bolt snapping back penetrated his senses. Then a moment later he saw the door swinging inward, cautiously.

A gun muzzle was poked around the edge, and then above

it the cruel face of a guard. Thick lips grinned and the door was flung wide. Beyond the burly form of the guard, Dusty saw the man he hated with all the intensity of his entire being—the Black Hawk.

Motioning the guard to step aside and let him pass, the Hawk advanced toward Dusty and stood staring down at him. A second later his eyes flickered toward Agent 10, and his smile broadened.

"He had his choice, to talk or die."

The rasping voice made Dusty's blood boil, but a strange silent warning that rippled through him forced him to remain motionless. He slumped back against the wall and relaxed completely.

"That's something your breed could never understand!" he said evenly. "But get this, Black Hawk. That man was my friend. I've promised him your life, and I never go back on a promise!"

Perhaps it was the utter lack of boastfulness in the Yank's tone, or perhaps it was the determination that gleamed deep in his eyes—but at any rate the Hawk's ugly face paled for the fraction of a second. Then he threw back his head and roared with laughter.

"A THREAT and a promise, eh?" he snorted. Then bending close, "And how do you plan to keep your promise when in the matter of a few hours you, too, will be dead? Did you think that because you talked, I'm going to let you go free? You, who have annoyed me so much?"

In spite of himself, Dusty sat up straight.

"What the hell do you mean, I talked?" he thundered.

The other pointed toward the dead man.

"Did he not tell you?" he asked. Then answered his own question. "But no, he had not regained consciousness then. Of course you talked, Captain. There is no longer anything for you to tell me."

Dusty grinned at him scornfully.

"That line won't work!" he bit off. "I wouldn't tell you the time, and neither you nor your whole rotten gang could ever make me."

The Hawk smiled. "Did you not know that a man in a semi-conscious, delirious state of mind quite often babbles out things that under normal conditions he would keep to himself?

"Well, Captain, that is exactly what you did. Yes, the guard who struck you with his gun will be rewarded well."

Dusty struggled to his feet and half fell against the wall. Fighting to keep himself up, he glared at the man.

"You lie!" he bellowed.

The Hawk, the gloating expression on his face proving he was thoroughly enjoying himself, watched the Yank's determined efforts to remain on his feet.

"No!" he suddenly spat out. "You told me what I wanted to know. You wildly cursed yourself for not having sent word to your G.H.Q. when you had the chance!"

Like the thunder of doom the man's words beat against Dusty's whirling brain.

The Hawk saw the bitter chagrin on the Yanks face, and his own became almost inhuman in its expression of insane triumph.

"For your efforts," he said, "you deserve a reward. You are the only American who knows of our great plan to crush your country. All the others who knew are now dead.

"And so, Captain, I shall let you live long enough to watch our final and lasting triumph. As my reluctant guest you will fly with me and witness the doom of your country. Come!"

For an instant Dusty hesitated. Desire to go down fighting right then and there swept over him. He swayed crazily on his feet. And then, as the Hawk's gun suddenly popped into view, he went deadly calm and grinned inwardly as a crazy idea flashed through his brain. A moment later he nodded, and put one bracing hand against the wall.

"Okay," he mumbled. "Okay. But don't rush—I'm—all in. I give up—you win. Hell!"

Hating himself for it, he forced a whimpering groan off his lips. The Hawk sneered and took hold of his arm.

"When it is too late," he mocked as they went through the door, "the fool gets a little sense in his head!"

Dusty made no answer. Eyes narrowed against a brilliant sunshine that greeted him, and lungs sucking in cool fresh air, he stumbled forward like a drunken man, letting his weight sag on the other's arm.

Guiding his charge to the right, the Hawk started along behind the line of hangars. Still faking a state of near collapse, Dusty cast his eyes furtively about. An instant later his heart leaped as he saw the guard who had entered the prison block with the Hawk, salute stiffly and run on ahead toward the tail of a Black attack plane that was just visible beyond the corner of the end hangar.

And a few moments later Dusty had a feeling of exultation as he saw that the field was practically deserted. At least there were no mechanics within a hundred yards of them.

One last final play in this game of death. The odds were all against him. But, hell, he couldn't lose anything except his own life, now. And his life wouldn't be worth living, if he muffed this last chance.

Breathing hoarsely, he tripped over his own feet, fell down on one knee, then struggled up with a sobbing moan.

"Wait—wait please!" he choked out, letting his body pivot slowly around. "Let me—get my breath—a second."

The Hawk stopped and sneered at him.

"So the courageous one has broken at last?" he grated.

"Sorry," mumbled Dusty as he shot a quick look toward the attack plane. "God—my chest hurts so!"

HE RAISED a hand to his chest and groaned. The Black's eyes left his face and looked down. And in that instant Dusty staked his last bet against the Grim Reaper.

Every ounce of his strength left in him, he put into his right hand that shot out and grasped the Hawk's gun wrist. In the same instant he whipped up his right knee to the man's stomach.

The Black snarled and tried to jerk back, but the snarl was lost in a grunt of pain as Dusty's knee found its mark and his other hand twisted the gun free. The next instant he had the gun jammed against the Hawk's ribs.

"Now, you dance," he husked savagely. "I'm itching to do this—for Agent 10. I promised him, you know. A nice little slug ripping through your rotten hide. They tell me that a bullet in the stomach hurts like hell. Want to find out?"

"You'll die for this!"

The words were hissed off cruel lips that were now trembling in stark fear. And fear shone in the sunken, black eyes.

"Maybe I will," said Dusty, crowding close, so it would look as though the other still supported him. "But you'll go first. Nothing can stop me from slapping a slug into your guts.

"Now, listen, we're going over to that ship. Keep close to me—like this. Feel the gun right smack against you? And when we get close to the ship, order that guard of yours to the other end of the hangar line. And do it in English, get me? In English! So help me—one dizzy word or sign and you get it. And, that is a promise!"

The Hawk tried desperately to sneer. But the look in Dusty's eyes checked the attempt. The Black was looking into eyes of death, and he knew it. For one second more he hesitated, then he wilted as he seemed to sense Dusty's finger tightening on the trigger. Slowly he started toward the end hangar.

"You will die for this!" he got out from between grinding teeth.

"Then I'll be seeing you," Dusty grunted, sticking close to him.

Eyes alert for any untoward movement, the Yank forced the Hawk down to the end of the hangar line. His heart was thumping madly, and his hand gripping the gun was clammy.

Each split second was an eternity of hellish waiting for an expectant voice to cry out in back of him, or Black soldiers to come running around the corner of the hangar. If either happened, he had no idea what he would do. He only knew that no matter what might happen to him, the Black Hawk would breathe his last breath this side of hell.

Fifty feet from the plane—forty feet! Dusty felt the Hawk's body stiffen. He dug the gun muzzle into the man's ribs.

"Remember!" he breathed out the corner of his mouth. "You get it first. A hot slug where it will hurt the most!"

Faking a slight stumble, Dusty lurched against the Hawk and made him walk around the tail of the plane, so that the fuselage came between him and the guard. Through slitted eyes he saw the guard watching them intently. There was a puzzled expression on the man's face. Dusty jabbed the gun muzzle deeper, and half turned so that the guard could not see his lips.

"Order him away!" he breathed softly, eyes riveted on the Hawk's face. "Order him away—in English!"

For a split second heaven and earth seemed to stand still. And Dusty held his breath. If the Hawk refused—

"Go to my quarters, and wait for me!"

THE HAWK had spoken! Dusty stood rigid, gun jammed in the Black's ribs, and eyes glued to his ugly face. Behind him he heard heels click, then footsteps on the concrete tarmac.

For one second Dusty took a quick look out the corner of his eye.

The guard was thirty yards down the tarmac, walking sidewise, face turned toward them.

"Stand still!" he grated as the Hawk's body trembled with helpless rage. "For your sake, I hope the boy friend doesn't get

AS THE PLANE LEAPED FORWARD
HE SAW THE HAWK'S UNCONSCIOUS
FIGURE GO SWEEPING OFF ONTO
THE GROUND....

curious. Guess the English order surprised him. Well, don't let him come back. I could get you both—easy!"

The Hawk muttered something under his breath, and his arms pinned helpless by Dusty's fake collapse position jerked spasmodically. But the Yank only grinned and pulled him over to where the cockpit domed up and hid them both from the guard.

Then Dusty released his hold, stepped back, but kept the gun trained on the Hawk. Then, shooting a quick side glance at the double cockpit, he shook his head and grunted.

"Nope," he said, as though talking to himself. "Can't waste the time. I was going to let you be my guest. But I can't chance it. So open that door. I said, open that cockpit door!"

Face twisted with rage, the Black reached out and jerked open the door. Dusty took a step toward it, then stopped and fixed agate eyes on the man. His hand gripping the gun went white at the knuckles.

"I think I'll keep that promise now!" he said tightly. "It wouldn't be murder. Killing a rotten rat isn't murder."

The Hawk's eyes went glassy, and his jaw sagged. Dusty eyed him scornfully, and moved the gun an inch or so nearer. But something inside of him refused to let him pull the trigger. Besides a shot might bring others over on the run—and he couldn't risk a general fight right now. He cursed softly.

"Nope, I think I'll give you a break this time!" he snapped. "You can live a while and tell that guard who socked me, just what a clout on the head feels like!"

As the last rushed off his tongue, he swung the gun up and

put every bit of his weight behind the blow. The Hawk, who was heaving a sigh of relief, saw the gun slicing up too late. It caught him just behind the right ear.

Stiff as a ramrod he started over backward, but Dusty grabbed him and let him fall across the lower wing of the ship. Then, making sure that the man's feet and legs would look as though he were lounging against a strut, he slipped into the cabin cockpit and closed the door. His trained eyes swept over the mass of strangely marked instruments, and for an instant he frowned in perplexity. But almost immediately he found the gadgets he wanted; opened the throttle, snapped up the ignition switch, and jammed his foot down on the electric starter.

A second or two of hellish tension dragged by, then the foreign engine, cowled in the nose, caught and roared into full-throated life. Slapping off the wheel brakes, Dusty breathed a prayer and heeled the throttle all the way open. As the plane leaped forward he saw the Hawk's unconscious figure go sweeping off onto the ground, and then it was lost to view.

"Don't worry!" he thundered into the howl of the engine. "I'll be back to keep my promise!"

Fifty yards out on the field the wheels cleared, sank back onto the ground, and then cleared again. Faintly he heard the savage bark of ground-pit guns, and the sharp twang as unseen wasps ricocheted off the metal fuselage.

The Hawk's body had been seen, and the field crew was trying to cut the Yank off. Eyes agate, body hunched over the stick, he poked the ship skyward and held his breath as he went, charging through a hail of whining death.

CHAPTER 12
HELL TRAP

UP, UP, up he went, the hollow steel prop clawing frantically at the air, and the engine straining every nut and bolt to drive to even greater speed. He did not level off until he was lost in a cloud bank. And only then, so that he could get his compass bearings and veer around toward the south.

Till now the joy of escape had been uppermost in his mind, but as he oozed up through the cloud bank and into clear air again, fingers of ice clutched at his heart anew, and his mouth went dry and burning.

His way was free, yes. And there was a stout ship under him. But between him and home was a smoking, flaming wall of war. The southern horizon was completely blanketed out by gas and smoke-screen curtains.

And darting and twisting through them were countless ships of both Black and American forces. Through them he would be forced to fly. The Blacks first, and then through a swarm of his own countrymen.

Even as he debated the chances of flying around them to the east or the west, he saw three Black Darts cut away from a dogfight and swing around toward him.

His guess was as good as the truth. He knew it, and his heart sank. The field staff on the Hawk's drome had already radioed his escape. And now the Hawk's brood were closing in to cut down the conqueror of their leader.

"What did you expect—a free ride home?"

The sudden sound of his voice startled him, then steadied him, firm as a rock. He tore his eyes from the onrushing ships for a second, looked at the trigger trips on the stick and grinned. The Blacks and the Yanks had at least one thing in common— they both fired their guns the same way.

A second later he reached out his free hand to the radio panel, spun the wave-length knob, and clamped the phones over his head. The result made the grin on his face disappear altogether.

A high-keyed hum in the phones told him that he was in a static-jammed area. For reasons he didn't know, but could perfectly well guess, the Blacks had static-jammed their side of the lines, after sending the warning ahead.

"That's that!" he grunted. "It's through you go, kid. And hope for luck on the other side!"

Deliberately allowing the Black ships to get in close, he held his plane on a level, dead-on course, until the others were almost on top of him. Then, as their pointed noses began to spit twin streams of jetting flame, he thumped rudder to the right, jammed on opposite rudder almost immediately and pulled the stick back into his stomach.

The Blacks, expecting a tricky zoom attack from beneath, pulled out to the side. Before they realized what was happening, Dusty was plunging into the cloud bank, engine wide open. Like a bullet he went through it, and out of it into clear air. But even then he didn't pull out.

Engine thundering, wings virtually groaning in protest again the excess strain, he held the ship dead-on for the ground.

THE PURPLE TORNADO

The altimeter needle on the dash slid like the second hand of a watch. Four thousand, three thousand, two thousand—one thousand!

Below, scattered groups of Black soldiers stared up in utter amazement at some pilot who couldn't possibly avoid plunging headlong into the ground. Four hundred feet, and still diving. That man was mad, crazy—or was he dead?

Such must have been the thoughts of those bewildered Blacks. But that steel-clawed eagle at the stick was neither mad nor dead. Instinct had led him to the one way out, a wild, hedge-hopping race southward, and he was taking it at peak speed.

High above him, three Black pilots twisted their ships, seeking a glimpse of their prey who had dodged into the clouds, waiting for him to show himself, and die. And then too late, they realized that they had been tricked again.

Far below them, hugging the tree tops, miles ahead, was their prey. As Dusty jerked his head around and looked up, he saw them slide into V formation and climb up through the cloud bank.

As he turned front again there was a happy grin on his wan and blood-drawn face. So far, so good. Twenty minutes and an equal amount of luck, and he'd be on the American side.

IT WAS less than twenty minutes—twelve and a half to be exact. But to him it was a lifetime spent in hell. A hell made up of roaring guns, seething flame and heavy enveloping gas clouds.

But he did not flinch for one instant. It was a gauntlet of life and death, and the fire of the fighter within him flared up with an all-consuming intensity. A race against time—

The attack on the Z-10 area had been started twelve hours ahead. Was the attack on the Buffalo area and New York underway now?

Plunging through flaming air, he fought desperately with himself as to where he should land and spread the alarm.

Time meant everything. He had wasted all he could afford to. It might even be too late now.

Beyond this hell of smoke and flame, and singing shells that made his ship rock and buck as they whammed by, were American troops. But what good would it be to tell them of the great danger at Buffalo and New York? They had enough danger on their hands, right where they were.

It was the reinforcements rushing up that he must head off. He must stop that great doomed army that was being sucked up into a gigantic trap. Once they were up there—

He banished the rest from his brain as he went charging out of the curtain of purple and red hell, and over Yank-occupied ground.

Beneath his wings, American gunners were hurling steel death into the Black's defenses, and the ground literally crawled with puppet tanks going forward in front of infantry waves. A great grotesque fighting machine charging head-on into another machine equally grotesque in appearance.

It was not until he was several miles back of the first wave that he saw human faces. The thousands going into the battle had been hidden by gas masks and flame suits. And behind them, thousands more were preparing to take their places.

Gripped by the spell of the horrible scene that seemed to spread out to the four horizons, Dusty was unable to jerk himself out of it until a shower of steel from American guns slashed up at him.

He had forgotten what minutes before he had fully expected. Americans—his comrades in arms—were blazing away at what they believed to be an enemy plane.

And a second later the telltale tac-a-tac-tac from above, drummed against his ears. As he glanced up and saw the four Yank pursuits piling down, guns flaming, he shot out his free hand and turned up full volume of the radio.

"I'm Ayres!" he bellowed into the transmitter. "Captain Ayres… a Yank. Lead me to the nearest main area H.Q. Which way?"

The phones crackled.

"Like hell! You can't fool us. Land in that field a mile south."

In blind desperation Dusty banged his free fist against the side of the cockpit.

"I am Ayres… Captain Ayres, you dumbbell… for God's sake, the nearest main area H.Q. quick! It's important!"

For an answer, a savage burst of fire cut across the nose of Dusty's plane.

"That's a last warning!" the phones barked. "You can't get away with it. Land, I'm telling you. My fingers are getting itchy!"

Dusty groaned, and for one wild instant he elected to take a chance and drive through this bunch of nitwits.

But as they closed in around him, he killed the urge. They'd never let him get through—not that bunch, whoever they were. He didn't recognize their markings. Nope, dammit, it was best to land.

Jerking the throttle back, he sent the ship sliding down toward an infantry camp, close to the field the strange pilot had indicated and as the plane slid down, he spun the wave-length knob furiously.

"Washington… Washington H.Q… Captain Ayres calling!"

But his only answer was a sharp crackling in the phones. The escorting pursuits were on his wave-length, and he couldn't get through to Washington.

And then, before he could plead with them to get off, his wheels touched and he braked to a savage stop.

SLAMMING OPEN the door he leaped out and ran headlong for the leading pursuit floating down. As it rolled to a stop, and the cockpit cowling was slid back, he leaped up on the fuselage step and grabbed a wide-eyed, and thoroughly dumbfounded lieutenant.

"Now, damn you!" he roared. "Out of this ship… I'm taking it for a while!"

The other continued to gape at him.

"My God!" he finally blurted out. "You are Captain Ayres. But—but we heard that you were dead. It came over the radio. And you're hurt, Captain!"

Dusty curled his fingers in the man's tunic and jerked him up.

"Out!" he roared. "I'm in a hurry! Where's the main area H.Q.? Speak up, man—speak up!"

The other virtually fell out of his ship, assisted considerably by Dusty.

"Listen, that's my ship, Captain!" he gulped. "I'm responsible for it. And there isn't any main area H.Q. It's a mobile unit attack. And I—"

"Here, what the devil's all this about?"

Dusty turned to stare into the puffing red face of an infantry general. Behind him trailed a few staff johnnies.

"I'm General Conklin!" he wheezed as he came to a halt. "What happened to you?"

"You can help me, sir," Dusty cut him off excitedly. "I've got to get word through to G.H.Q. This attack here is a fake. The Blacks are planning to smash through the Buffalo area—maybe they've started already. And you'll all be trapped!"

"What?" the other roared at him. "You call this a fake attack? You damn fool, who are you anyway?"

"Captain Ayres!" the pilot told him. "And for God's sake, sir, help me to get through to G.H.Q. The troops coming north must be stopped. The Buffalo area, and—"

"Funny!" the general said. "We were in the Buffalo area twelve hours ago, and it was as quiet as could be. Anyway, you can't get G.H.Q. now. The whole General Staff is on its way up here by special train."

Dusty saluted.

"Thank you, sir. Excuse me—I'm in a hurry."

"Here, wait a minute! Where the devil are you going? I say, Captain?"

But Dusty wasn't listening. Before any of them could bat an eyelash, he leaped into the plane and rammed the throttle wide open. A cloud of dirt-filled prop-wash swept them all off their feet.

And as they swore and dug at their half blinded eyes, Dusty pulled the ship clear and went screaming up into the air.

Slamming around past the other Yank ships that were now floating in to land, he cut sharp to the south and gave the engine every drop of hop juice it could take.

"Can't get G.H.Q. now, eh?" he roared savagely. "Well, we'll damned well find about that!"

As the last ripped off his lips he snapped up the radio panel switch and turned the wave-length knob to the S.O.S. Emergency reading. Then slapping the phones over his head, he grabbed up the transmitter.

"General Staff train, en route!" he shouted. "Calling General Staff train, en route. Important. Give me your position at once. This is Captain Ayres calling from the air. My map reading position approximately J-34. Give me your position. I have important information. Emergency... emergency... emergency!"

With baited breath he glued his eyes to the signal light on the instrument board. It seemed as though he died a thousand deaths before it finally blinked, and a voice spoke in the phones.

"Orders of commanding general! All stations will remain off this wave-length for thirty minutes. Until then make all reports to your unit commander!"

Gritting his teeth, Dusty stepped up the volume.

"This is Captain Ayres!" he bellowed. "I've got to contact General Staff. If you can't listen in, tell me where in hell you are!"

With tantalizing monotony the voice in the earphones droned back at him.

"Repeating order of commanding general. All stations will keep off this wave-length for...."

"Shut up and listen to me!" howled Dusty. "My God, do you want to lose the damned war?"

"... make all reports to your unit commander. Signing off."

With a groan the pilot leaned back against the head rest, and glared into space. Then suddenly he sat up straight and turned the dial knob to another reading.

"Calling commanding officer of Buffalo Area! Calling commanding officer of Buffalo Area... on wave-length 2, 7, 8. Please plug in on me at once... it's important!"

Seconds dragged by, became one minute, then two. Voice trembling with rage, Dusty repeated his call three times. Halfway through the fourth time the red light blinked and a booming voice roared in the phones, "Wave length 2, 7, 8... get the devil off the air! You're jamming up everything. This is Major Trapp, General Staff adjutant speaking! Get off, 2, 7, 8... and stay off!"

"Like hell I will!" roared Dusty and stepped transmission volume up to peak. "This is Captain Ayres. I must talk with you. It's important!"

"Captain Ayres?" exploded the phones. "You're crazy. Ayres is dead. Now, by God get off, before you get into trouble."

The light winked out.

"Of all the damned, fat-headed nitwits!" Dusty thundered.

Reaching out his free hand, he snapped off the set switch.

"Okay, okay," he muttered grimly. "Have it your way. But, I'm still going to find you. I started this thing, and by God I'll finish it!"

SWEEPING DOWN below a thin cloud layer, he checked his position on the roller map on the dash, and then started a wide, zigzag course south, down the heart of New Hampshire and across the Massachusetts line.

But every mile he flew was a mile of raging chagrin. Below him the might of America's fighting forces were sweeping northward. Every rail-line was clogged with one-way troop and equipment traffic.

And it was the same all along the network of broad highways. Which of those countless troop trains contained the General Staff? The more he peered down at them the more helpless seemed his task.

And then, suddenly, he sat bolt upright in the seat. Off to his right, and slightly northwest of Worcester, he saw several troop trains easing into sidings, and leaving the main line clear.

Snatching up his binoculars, he trained them on the main line and followed it south. A minute later a shout of joy burst from his lips.

Just south of the Massachusetts line a three-car armored train was speeding northward at breakneck speed. One look and he knew it to be the General Staff train. It was getting the right of way, while the fighting forces waited in sidings for it to go by.

Sticking the nose of his plane down, Dusty headed right for it like a thunderbolt out of the blue. He met it just north of Springfield. Swooping low he throttled to its speed and buzzed back and forth across the heavily armored roof. And as he did he snapped on the radio.

"This is Ayres again!" he yelled. "The Blacks are going to attack at...."

The last was choked off as a gun turret just back of the streamlined nose of the train spat jetting flame at him. With a curse he dodged to the side then cut down so that he was racing forward on a level with the steel-framed, bulletproof windows. Slamming back the cockpit cowl he half raised himself from the seat and waved frantically at the dimly outlined faces inside the windows.

"The Blacks!" he shouted. "The Blacks are going to attack at Buffalo. It's a trick—a trick! For God's sake stop the general movement north. I tell you, you'll be swamped!"

And the answer he got was a double blast of machine-gun fire from the two ends of the train. An instinctive movement on the controls and a pilot's luck was all that saved him from getting a shower of steel in his face. Cursing and shouting, he zoomed up and tore forward along the track.

Ten miles north, his blazing eyes found what they had been seeking—a grade crossing that was wide enough, and without gates.

"By God, you boneheads, will you listen to me yet?" he grated, and swung out in a wide turn.

Cutting the throttle, he swung back just over the highway. Then with a steady hand he eased the ship down foot by foot.

It was a tricky job as both sides of the highway were lined with tall trees. But his calculating eyes had seen the three-foot clearance on each end of his wingtips, and to him three feet were as good as three miles.

Lower and lower he sank, gaging his descent to a fine hair. At the crossing a flagman was doing all sorts of acrobatics to attract his attention, and to the south he heard the faint scream of the staff train's siren. But he paid no attention to either. Every part of him was concentrated on making a perfect dead-stick landing.

And then, finally, his wheels touched fifteen feet from the crossing. Stick all the way back to hold the tail down, he let the plane roll forward until it was right smack in the middle of the crossing. Then he thumped down on the brake pedals, and stopped the roll dead.

"You damned fool. You damned fool! Do you want to wreck it? There's a staff train coming. Get this thing out of here."

The flagman had climbed up on the fuselage step, and was screaming words at him through frothing lips. With a quick motion, Dusty flung him off and legged out. The flagman was beside himself with rage.

"You'll wreck the staff train. You'll wreck it—"

Dusty clapped a hand over the man's mouth and pulled him off the crossing.

"I hope to hell I do, if they don't stop!" he snapped. "Look out—here she comes!"

CHAPTER 13
THE PURPLE TORNADO

ITS METAL sides and roof gleaming, the Staff train poked its streamlined snout around a bend half a mile away and came rushing down the track. For several hellish seconds Dusty held his breath in fear and dread. Were the damned fools going to chance being derailed and plow right through?

His heart like a lump of ice in his chest, he kept one hand over the fuming, gurgling flagman's mouth, and glued his eyes to the train. On it rushed, a steel-clad juggernaut on wheels. It wasn't going to stop! It was going right—

Suddenly, air brakes screeched horribly. But to Dusty's ears it was music. Swaying crazily, the train slackened its plunging speed foot by foot. Wheels ground on the rails, and coupling joints clanged and banged together. And finally, its snout not more than twenty yards from the crossing, the train came to a dead stop.

Seconds later all hell broke loose. Doors and windows banged open and a swarm of O.D. clad figures, headed by the grease smeared train crew, came pounding down to the crossing. The air was filled with a hundred curses, and shouted questions.

For a moment Dusty was buried in a swirling tangle of arms and clutching hands. Eventually; the roaring voice of Colonel Marberry blasted loudest in Dusty's ears.

"Good God—Ayres! I told you, General. I didn't believe it. Ayres, this is General Cummings, Chief of Staff!"

A big, white-mustached man with blazing eyes confronted Dusty.

"What's the meaning of this, Captain? Was that you blocking out wave-length? Was—?"

Something snapped in Dusty's brain. He grabbed the general by the tunic lapels and shook him vigorously.

"Shut up, sir, and listen to me! The Z-10 area attack is a fake. A trick to draw you all up north, so that the Blacks can crash through at Buffalo—and at New York by sea. I—"

"Wait a minute—stop!" the senior officer thundered. "Major Trapp, have the crew pull the plane off the track. Colonel Marberry, come with me to my car and we'll hear what Ayres has to say. I'll give the order to proceed later."

Turning his back on them, the general stamped down the train side to his car. Dusty followed at his heels. Colonel Marberry and several others brought up the rear. And it was not until they were all seated in the car compartment that the general finally unsealed Dusty's lips.

"Now, Captain," he said, fixing him with steely eyes, "tell us what this is all about. A supposedly dead man coming to life, rather amazes me, to say the least."

Steadying his temper, Dusty sucked in a deep breath and started to talk, slowly. He told them step by step everything that had happened. But as he talked his anger mounted, and before long he was leaning over the table and pounding home his truths with blood-smeared fists.

THE PURPLE TORNADO

SUDDENLY, AIR BRAKES SCREECHED HORRIBLY.

"And all of that is fact, sir!" he finished up. "You're riding right smack into the biggest trap ever set. Half a dozen brave men have already died, trying to check the thing; and you owe it to them, to believe me. It's truth, sir. And I've been trying to tell it to you for over an hour, but you wouldn't stay on my wave-length!"

Completely exhausted, the pilot sank back on his seat, eyes still clamped on the general's face. For a moment heavy silence settled over the compartment room. Eventually, General Cummings coughed throatily and scowled at his folded hands.

"**I WOULD** believe you, Captain," he said testily. "Except for a few facts that we happen to know ourselves. The Navy Department reports that the entire Black North Atlantic fleet is moving down on the main coast. And our coast patrol reports not a single Black ship has been sighted within a hundred miles of New York.

"The fact that we've been keeping in touch with navy maneuvers, and the fact that we had received a definite report from Second Infantry that you and General Billings had been killed by spies, explains why we did not let you contact us. But, aside from that, my reports from our entire line state that there is action in only the Z-10 area! And—"

Dusty suddenly leaned forward.

"When did you get them?"

"When?" the other echoed angrily. "Why, early this morning. When I ordered our general reserves to move north. The exact time, I believe, was about four o'clock."

As the general finished, Dusty shot out his hand and grabbed his wrist.

"Look, sir!" Dusty cut him off, pointing at the man's wrist watch. "It's four in the afternoon. Twelve hours! Don't you see?"

The general glared at him.

"What in the hell are you talking about?"

"This!" Dusty shouted at him. "The Z-10 attack was started twelve hours ahead of time. Why, I don't know. Maybe the Blacks got anxious. Or maybe that army moving southwest behind the lines got to the Buffalo area ahead of time.

"But, there were to be twenty-four hours between the two attacks. And the end of that twenty-four hours is right now! The Buffalo attack is starting—now!"

The senior officer started to speak, then clapped his lips shut. Colonel Marberry leaned toward him.

"I agree with Captain Ayres, sir," he said quietly. "I would suggest that we contact Buffalo and New York and find out what they have to report."

"Check!" said Dusty before he could stop himself.

General Cummings' face went beet red.

"Young man," he thundered, "I order you to keep a more civil tongue in your head! I haven't liked your tone from the beginning!"

"I'm sorry, sir," the pilot replied evenly. "But, I can't help thinking of the men I saw die for their country! I earnestly beg of you to do as Colonel Marberry suggests."

It seemed to Dusty that every man in the room held his

breath, while the general scowled some more at his folded hands. Then, presently, he nodded his head sadly.

"Very well," he got out gruffly. "It won't take up much more of our time. Lieutenant Allen, use my official code signal and contact both New York and Buffalo for immediate reports!"

A slim, flaxen-haired officer said, "Very well, sir," and disappeared through a door leading to an adjoining compartment.

A moment later they all heard the faint sound of his voice speaking into the transmitter. Dusty sat rigid, eyes fixed on the table, a sense of bitter weariness was creeping over him. He felt as though he were beating his fists helplessly against a steel wall.

Through fire and death he had come with his warning. And now, here at the end of his trail, he had run into a stubborn "Medal-rack" who had to be virtually bulldozed into the smallest bit of action. What a person to put in command of the lives of four million fighting men! Hell!

Then, suddenly, his brooding revery was shattered as Lieutenant Allen came dashing into the compartment.

"General!" he called. "Captain Ayres must be right. I can't get any reply from New York. And Buffalo's signals faded out just as they began to talk. Something has happened on both ends."

OF ALL those in the room, General Cummings was the least excited. In fact, he seemed just a trifle disappointed that something queer had happened. He glared at his officers.

"Probably only temporary," he said almost sullenly. Then to Allen, "You tried relaying my orders?"

The young officer nodded.

"Yes, sir, via Cleveland, also Pittsburgh. But neither has checked back with me. I—"

The man stopped short as sound came from the speaker unit beyond the half-closed door.

"Cleveland calling General Staff, enroute, on 2, 7, 8. Unable to contact Buffalo area station as ordered. Something seems wrong at their end. Will keep trying and check back to you as soon as contact has been made."

There was the click of the Cleveland station signing off. But before anyone in the compartment could speak, the radio made sound again.

"Pittsburgh calling General Staff, enroute on 2, 7, 8. No reply from Buffalo or New York. Unusual oscillation, but no signals. Check back in five minutes. Going off."

"They've started! And now they've static-jammed both sections from the air. They could do it easily with the equipment I saw headed that way!"

Dusty paused long enough to catch his breath.

"Now, sir, will you stop the general movement north?" he pleaded. "There's the proof you need!"

General Cummings shook a finger at him.

"Any more of your insubordination. Captain," he thundered, "and I'll have you put under arrest! Proof you say? I certainly demand more proof than that, before I'll change the maneuvers of over two million men and arms!"

"Then may I make a suggestion, sir?" asked Dusty. And before the other could reply, "I can make the Buffalo area in less than an hour—and get proof. If the attack has started, or is about to, I'll use your official code signal and warn every ground station within range. And you, picking up my signals, can warn all those my set may not reach. It's our one chance, sir!"

"He's absolutely right, sir!" cut in Colonel Marberry, before Cummings had a chance to open his thin-lipped mouth. "We can't afford to take further risks. The danger's too great. As an appointed member of the General Staff I insist that we make sure immediately, the way Captain Ayres suggests. Here, Captain, I'll help you get away."

As the colonel dragged him out of the compartment, Dusty had the flash impression of General Cummings' jaw slowly sagging open, and the faint pleased grin on the face of each of the others. Then he was running along the tracks toward his plane, Colonel Marberry's hurried words drifting back to him.

"I believe you, Ayres, and I'm going to risk my neck and career because I do. The general is of the old school, and difficult at times. But this time we've got to chance the consequences."

The officer paused for breath and didn't speak again until Dusty was legging into the plane.

"Sure you can make it?" he asked anxiously. "You look ready to flop right now. Perhaps—"

"Flop now, sir?" the pilot echoed happily. "Hell, I'm just getting started. Sir, I told the general that I'd send out a warning. Well, if the attack has started I won't be sending out any warning. I'll be ordering the reinforcements back, and using the General

Staff code signal! Hell, I should have done it long ago, instead of wasting time reporting to him!"

"Right!" the other nodded as Dusty reached for the throttle. "Good luck, lad, And by the way, most of Staff is different. It was his idea to drive away a pesky aviator whom he thought was strafing his train. None of us ordered the men to fire on you."

"Don't worry, sir," Dusty grinned, "I knew that he'd pulled that stunt as soon as I met him. S'long."

A quick glance forward to make sure that the members of the train crew had stepped aside, and Dusty rammed the throttle wide open. Like a shot from a gun the plane leaped forward, bounced across the rough crossing, and went careening off to the right.

The pilot ruddered it clear and lifted it into the air. As he went up through the narrow space between the bordering trees, a branch slapped against the right wing. But with his speed, and with a final upward lunge, he roared into the open.

Leveling off at an even thousand feet, he set a dead-on course for the Buffalo area, hunched himself over the stick and strained his eyes ahead. Low hanging clouds obscured his view for several minutes.

But as the plane thundered west across the Massachusetts-New York line he thought he saw a queer, dull haze low down on the horizon. And as he raced toward it the haze seemed to spread out, and become almost jet-black in color. A great black mushroom growing bigger and bigger with each passing moment.

And then, as he tore through a thin intervening cloud layer, his eyes met a sight that chilled him to the core. The mushroom was not black, as it had seemed through the cloud layer. It was deep purple in color, and no longer mushroom in shape.

In fact, Dusty's first impression was that a tornado of purple dust was rushing down across the narrow strip of Canadian ground between Lake Erie and Lake Ontario. Though still several miles from it, he could see it swirl and curl upward from an ever widening base, sweeping forward.

A few moments later he saw balls of fire rain down on the district of Buffalo.

Like magic the entire surrounding area became blanketed by a great sea of flame and rolling smoke.

Outward and outward it rolled, enveloping everything in its path until it seemed as though Erie and Ontario were one great lake, covered over in the middle by that swirling, purple tornado.

Then, as Dusty saw the tiny figures of soldiers and civilians stumble and stagger beyond the fringe of the cloud, and collapse in writhing heaps, he knew that the blow had been struck. The Blacks had launched a preliminary gas barrage, and would soon start hammering through the thin line of American defenses.

But as he reached out his free hand to the radio panel, the heavens above him suddenly trembled with the savage yammer of machine-gun fire, and a swarm of jet black wings came tearing down.

Death was not through yet. Now, at this final moment it was still reaching out to slam him down into hopeless defeat.

CHAPTER 14
BLACK DEATH

FOR ONE split second, Dusty sat spellbound, staring up at the great vulture cavalcade thundering down. His ship seemed to wince as singing steel tore through it, and his hand reaching for the radio-dial jerked instinctively back to his gun trips. With a curse he snapped back to the radio panel.

"Tell them first," he bellowed at himself. "Tell them, and scrap these rats later!"

In one continuous movement he flicked up the switch, spun the dial to S.O.S. Emergency wave-length, and grabbed the transmitter. He opened his mouth to yell, but the words died in his throat. A high-keyed hum in the earphones made him groan instead. Glancing above he saw six powerful radio ships sweeping into position to form a wave-length blackout curtain between himself and the eastern seaboard. He was in a dead area as long as they were between him and the coast.

Forgetting the radio for a moment he cut sharply toward the north. At his heels a flight of sleek black Darts spat streams of jetting flame. His whole body burned with a savage desire to whirl around and give them a dose of their own medicine.

"Stick to your job!" he grated harshly. "Don't go off half-cocked."

Every nerve and muscle tensed, he held his mad headlong course to the north. Out the corner of his eye he could see the purple tornado eating its way deeper and deeper into New York State.

Helpless against overwhelming odds, the American troops were slowly giving ground. Fighting every inch of the way, and hundreds of them, to say nothing of the civilian population, were dropping in their tracks as that swirling hell overtook them. He didn't dare look back because he knew that he could not run away if he did. The sight would send him charging down to their aid.

But his one job at the moment was to summon stronger aid than he alone could render. His weapon was the radio, not his twin Brownings in the nose, or the bombs in the cockpit chutes. His voice streaking through the air along radio waves was the one salvation of a trapped army.

Grimly holding his ship on its course, he turned in the seat, glanced back, and grunted. It was now, or never.

Bracing himself he hauled back on the stick with all his might. The craft trembled, then went screaming up in a gigantic loop.

Three-quarters of the way over he kicked hard on the rudder, slammed the stick to the opposite corner, and jabbed both trigger trips. Guns spitting flame, the ship careened around in a lop-sided half roll.

Two Black Darts, closing in, went skidding away from the steel shower. Two more tried to hang on their props for a belly shot, but Dusty was now in a thundering dive to the southeast, and the hail of steel missed his wings by a good twenty yards.

The frantic maneuvers of the small pursuit planes didn't interest him a bit. His eyes were now glued to the radio planes high overhead. And as he saw them try to swing around in front of him a shout of triumph spilled off his lips, and he cut his dive sharp east.

TRICKED OUT of position, the radio planes were unable to keep up with him, and he went roaring past them and out of the dead area. Oblivious to the shower of death from pursuing guns, he grabbed the transmitter tube once more, and turned up full volume.

"S.O.S. Emergency... all American stations! Official Staff Code Signal G.P.H. Official Staff Code Signal G.P.H. Stand by for orders. Stand by for orders...."

Almost instantly the red light on the panel began to blink, and his heart leaped with joy. He was in clear air, and his signals were being received.

"Enemy breaking through Buffalo area!" he shouted wildly. "All units enroute to Z-10 change course and head southwest to cut off enemy attack in B-30 zone. Equip for gas and germ resistance. Enemy forces at maximum strength. All air units not engaged in actual combat elsewhere divide into groups for supporting ground defense at both B-30 zone and New York.

"Emergency... bear southeast of Buffalo area as it is now in the hands of enemy. Prepare to check attack in B-30 zone. Relay this order to adjoining units. Official Staff Code signal G.P.H. Official Staff Code signal G.P.H. Repeating order, five minute intervals!"

The earphones crackled with check-backs from a dozen different ground stations. So many in fact were clambering over the emergency wave-length that Dusty was unable to pick out a single signal.

But that didn't matter. His alarm had been received, and right now a steel fist would be swinging around to smash into that purple tornado behind him. But—and the thought chilled the blood in his veins—would that steel fist smash down too late?

For an instant he was inclined to change course and go back to the stricken area. But with an effort he curbed the idea. His job was not yet finished. He must still keep in clear air and repeat his order at five minute intervals. He—

A shower of steel-jacketed lead ripping through his right wingtip crystalized the decision. Behind him a skyful of black wings were trying to blast him out of the air. His lips slid back in a tight grin, and he went zigzagging crazily toward the east coast.

Five times he repeated his order. Struggling desperately to keep his ship clear of the spitting death which was licking out at him from three sides, he became a mechanical talking machine. And in his ears rattled the check-back signals from countless ground stations.

Then, suddenly, as he plunged through a section of heavy rain clouds and roared out into clear air, he choked off the order he was repeating, and shouted in alarm. For there, twenty miles ahead of him, was the city of New York—in flames!

At first glance it appeared like a gigantic torch of purple smoke and fire etched against the broad expanse of the Atlantic. But as he thundered toward it he was able to see the scene in detail.

Racing up and down the Hudson river front, their knife-like bows cleaving the churning waters, was a swarm of queer-looking armored motorboats. Great streams of crimson flame gushed out from a swivel nozzle mounted atop the cabin of each craft, and rainbows of dripping fire arced over burning ships and the piers and splashed against the buildings far beyond.

Overhead, supporting the strange fire-raiders, were whole squadrons of Black germ bombers and gas attack ships, pouring down their particular brand of hell upon the great city. And at lower altitude, sleek dart monoplanes were slicing down in between the towering buildings and spraying the panic-stricken multitudes with singing steel.

Like so many rats caught in a gigantic trap, civilians and home defense troops were being swallowed up by the seething red whirlpool. Every bridge across the East, Hudson and Harlem rivers had been reduced to twisted and crumpled metal that sagged down into frothing waters, running red with human blood.

Their main garrison troops having gone north, the Yank defenders were helpless against the steel tide. Coast batteries on Long Island and the Jersey shore were firing at almost point blank range at the fire spitting armored serpents streaking up and down the waterfront.

But only about one out of every hundred shells found its mark, and even then the damage wrought was slight.

A ring of anti-aircraft batteries about the city was desperately pumping death into the black-winged hordes above. And hopelessly bucking that hell on high were but two Yank pursuit squadrons from the eastern area. Just a handful of valiant eagles hurling themselves over the brink of certain doom.

STUNNED BY the terrible spectacle, Dusty sat rigid. New York, the greatest city on the face of the globe, was slowly being hammered into its own blood-soaked dust. The entire metropolitan area was doomed, unless—

God, where were the Yank forces? Where were the air units he had ordered to this zone? Had all the fools gone to the Buffalo area? That was a crash-through by land—troops could handle that. Planes were needed against this attack—bombers, pursuits, attacks, gas ships—everything!

With a wild shout, Dusty slammed his ship into a thundering dive, and grabbed up the transmitter.

"Stick with 'em, Yanks!" he bellowed. "Tear into 'em—we have help on the way! Stick it out until the reinforcements come! Give 'em hell, fellows!"

Whether the handful of Yank eagles heard him he didn't know, nor did he try to find out. Cursing he went streaking down into the yawning vortex of the red whirlpool.

His engine thundered to protest, and the wings groaned and trembled as a thousand steel trip-hammers smacked against them. The glass cockpit cowl melted into a million stinging splinters that whipped into the skin of his hands and face.

A lurch of the ship sent him crashing over against the cockpit side and ripped open the blood-caked gash on his forehead. Blood streamed down into his smarting eyes and half blinded him.

But his body was too engulfed by rage to sense any pain. Thumbs jammed against the trigger trips, he booted and slammed the plane about the smoking sky.

A black shadow raced across his sights, and instantly became a ball of fire. A third, a fourth, a fifth—Sane reason and caution tossed over the side, Dusty charged into anything with black wings. A thousand times over, death missed him by inches.

The metal covering of his wings became transformed into bullet-made sieves, and strips of the cowling ripped off and went skidding into the blood-red oblivion.

But he didn't notice, for he no longer had any thought for himself or his plane. He had no thought of anything except the twisting, turning, fire-spitting vultures all about him. Time became lost in that seething inferno. It was simply fight, fight, fight until he dropped.

And then, after what seemed like eternity dragged by, a human voice roared in the earphones.

"… and take circle formation. Bombers go down on the east. Attack ships from the south. Group numbers 12,4,16…."

As the voice droned on in the earphones, Dusty jerked himself up straight and stared dazedly about. He blinked hard, wiped blood drops from his eyes and looked again.

The heavens had become hammed with squadron after squadron of American planes. In line formation, group formation, and in V's, they were charging down upon the black-winged hordes. Bombers were swooping low over the rivers and dropping, roaring down upon the flame throwers.

And as Dusty jerked his eyes seaward he saw a squadron of Yank destroyers cutting the swells toward the entrance of the Narrows. Far behind them, low down on the northeastern horizon, was rolling smoke from the funnels of the bigger and slower ships.

Exultantly Dusty tore out to the rim of the fight and swung in along side a pursuit unit. But it wasn't until then that he saw the markings on the lead ship. He snatched up the transmitter.

"Hey, Major Drake. Hey, gang... it's me... Dusty... Dusty Ayres. Let's go to town!"

The lead ship swung around on wingtip, and Dusty's phones crackled.

"You, son? Well I'll be—"

"Look out, Major—look out!" called Dusty, as he saw a Black dart come zooming up from below. "A ship—under you!"

As he yelled the warning he slammed his plane down and cut in under the C.O. Instantly the Black ship fell over on wing and started to cut away.

But as it went over, Dusty saw the face of the pilot behind the glass cowling. It was the Black Hawk!

TAKEN BY surprise, he gaped blankly for a moment, and then as he saw Major Drake's plane go tearing down on the Black, he became a cursing, raving mad man.

"Major Drake—Drake!" he thundered into the transmitter. "I want to get that rat! I've been laying for him, sir!"

Like a meteor, he swept down past the C.O.'s plane and pounced on the Black, both guns yammering out a hymn of pent-up hate. Through red-filmed eyes he saw the Hawk turn in the seat and look back.

A split second later the Black plane cut sharply to the left and went streaking out across Long Island. Dusty laughed harshly and tore after him.

"No you don't!" he bellowed. "This time I deal the cards. Here, blast you, this is for Billings!"

Hot steel from his guns slashed into the tail of the other ship. It lurched crazily to the right. Like a flash Dusty was on it again.

"And this for Major Walker!"

Desperately the Hawk tried to skid clear, but Dusty's singing steel caught him square amidships. The Black plane fell over on wing. Then it spun around in a dime turn and charged straight for him, guns spitting flame.

"Come on, come on, you killer!" roared the Yank, jabbing the trips again. "This is for Strickland, and the radio sergeant. And some more for Major Shelton!"

Oblivious to the blazing fire from the other's guns, Dusty held his ship dead-on for the whirling prop. His eyes gleamed like balls of fire as he saw his bursts crash into the other plane.

It was the Hawk who finally weakened and cut away to avoid a mid-air crash. And that moment was the supreme climax of Dusty's entire life. He flung his ship down to the right. Then up and over he went—and down like a streak of light.

"And the last for Agent 10," he thundered. "For Agent 10—this and this—and this!"

Unable to slice clear of the charging plane, the Hawk nosed over and raced for the ground. But, even that was useless.

Clinging to the tail of the Black ship, Dusty poured bursts into it. And then, when the Black ship was but a bare hundred feet off the ground, the right wing let go, and the plane went cartwheeling crazily off to the right. Seconds later it became lost to view in a great cloud of smoky dust, as it hit on the edge of a small field.

Hardly conscious of what he was doing, the Yank slid down and landed close to the heap of crumpled wreckage. Stumbling out of the cockpit he staggered over and started tearing the wreckage aside.

"I'm making sure that you're dead," he grated. "I promised him—and by God, I'll keep that promise, I'll—"

He choked off the rest, as he pulled a slab of cowling clear and saw the figure pinned under the engine. Black eyes, seething flames in their depths, glared up at him. Cruel lips moved and a string of strange words screamed against Dusty's eardrums.

"The curse of my race is now upon you," the Hawk muttered savagely. "It will follow you to a swine's grave! It—"

The man stopped talking, and coughed raspingly. Blood spilled from his lips, and then with a spasmodic jerk he arched over backwards and went limp.

Holding onto a part of the crumpled wing for support, Dusty stared down into the cruel face for a long minute. Then slowly he raised his eyes skyward.

"I promised you, pal," he said thickly. "The Black Hawk's dead!"

And then as he started back toward his plane, the last thread of strength that had kept him going snapped. His knees buckled, and he collapsed on the ground.

Bracing his palms against the ground, he tried to get up. But his arms slipped out and he crashed down on his face as a great cloud of darkness engulfed him.

WHEN HE opened his eyes again he was swathed in bandages, and between the sheets of a hospital cot. Dully he stared at a blur just above him. Presently the blur cleared and became the grinning face of Major Drake. The C.O.'s lips were moving.

"How's it going, son?"

Dusty blinked, started to grin, then gasped. "I remember now—the attack! God, did they—Where's my clothes?"

The C.O. pushed him back on the pillow.

"Steady. You can't fight a one-man war every day in the week. Now, hold everything, and don't worry. What happened last week doesn't matter now. We—"

"Last week?" choked Dusty.

The other nodded.

"Eight days ago, to be exact. You were used up pretty well, you know. But, as I started to say, thanks to you we checked them at Buffalo with only a small loss of ground. And though a lot of New York is in ruins, it's still ours—and we can build it up.

"Incidentally, we gave their navy a neat beating, too. Part of it had been standing off shore, waiting for those damned flame-tossing motorboats to come back, and our boys trapped them."

The C.O. paused, and his face went grave.

"I pray to God we never have another close call like that again," he murmured. "If it hadn't been for you, if you hadn't spread the alarm—I don't even want to think of it!"

Dusty grated.

"I just had a couple of lucky breaks, sir," he said.

"That's what you say," grinned the other. "Don't worry, the whole country knows now what you went through, and did. And by the way, while you've been out you've been raving about the death of Agent 10. Well, you're wrong, Ayres. Agent 10 is alive."

Dusty stared at him in dumbfounded amazement.

"What?" he shouted. "Why, you're crazy! Agent 10 is dead—I saw him die. He—"

"No," the other shook his head. "Maybe you thought so, but he didn't. He escaped, got through the lines and is now in a Washington hospital recuperating."

The pilot heaved a happy sigh. "That is good news!" he breathed.

Drake grinned. "And here's some more good news," he added. "There are a flock of medals waiting for you. And—"

The C.O. paused and his grin widened.

"And General Cummings won't be the man who will pin them on your tunic."

The pilot shot him a questioning look. "What do you mean by that, sir?"

"Well," replied the other, shrugging his shoulders and pursing his lips, "stories get around, you know. And I have it from very good authority that General Cummings is being relieved of General Staff command.

"It seems that the War Department objects to a commanding general who has to have a fire-eating Air Force captain tell him how to run his army. Get what I mean?"

Dusty chuckled softly.

"I get it," he grunted. "And you can send those medals to the War Department, with my compliments!"

POPULAR PUBLICATIONS
HERO PULPS

LOOK FOR MORE SOON!

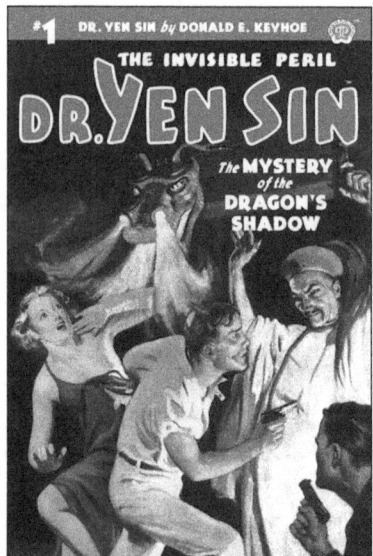

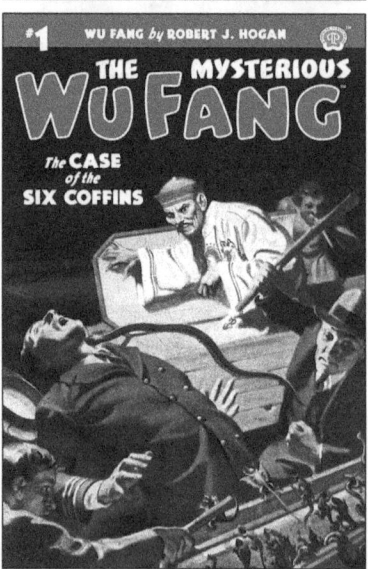